Queer middle-aged librarian Nan Nethercott, a wisecracking hypochondriac with a lackluster career and a nonexistent love life, needs to make a drastic life change before it's too late. When she lands a job as librarian in a seemingly idyllic small town in southern New Jersey, Nan quickly discovers unforeseen challenges.

Nan's landlady, Immaculata, launches daily intrusions from below. The library, housed in the former town jail, is overrun by marauding middle-schoolers. A mysterious reader leaves distressing messages in book stacks all over the library. Thomasina, the irresistible butch deli owner, is clearly a delicious affair and not the relationship Nan craves.

There's no turning back though. Nan must come up with her own wildly unorthodox solutions to what the town and its people throw at her and fight for what she wants until she makes a shiny new life—one with her first true home, surprising friends, a meaningful career, and a promising new love.

Here's to hope & laughter in all our days!

THE NEW

TOWN

LIBRARIAN

Kathy Anderson

KATHY ANDERSON

A NineStar Press Publication

www.ninestarpress.com

The New Town Librarian

© 2023 Kathy Anderson

Cover Art © 2023 Jaycee DeLorenzo

Edited by Elizabetta McKay

First Edition, January 2023

ISBN: 978-1-64890-608-4

Also available in eBook, ISBN: 978-1-64890-607-7

CONTENT WARNING:
This book contains sexual content, which may only be suitable for mature readers. Discussion of the death of a secondary character.

For my beloved book club for so many years of friendship, adventures, and support: Cathy Barnes, Donna Cameron, Mindy Sherman Gumminger, Gretchen Hall, and Suzanne Noll.

For librarians and library workers everywhere, fighting for our right to read.

"Of course it's alright for librarians to smell of drink."

—Barbara Pym, *Less Than Angels*

CHAPTER ONE

SO MANY DELIGHTFUL possibilities tonight. Nan Nethercott poured herself a hefty glass of red wine from the big box perched on her table and began.

Children's Librarian on Sanibel Island! Oh, to work in flip-flops and stroll the beach at lunchtime.

Research Librarian for the Irish Government in Dublin! She'd read lots of books set in Ireland. Surely that would count toward the requirement of a second master's degree in Irish history and fluency in Gaelic.

Film Archives Librarian in Hollywood! She loved movies. So what if she didn't have a background in art history with a film focus?

Cruise Ship Librarian! Ahoy, maties. Beach reads only.

Prison Librarian, Cuba! She focused on the Cuba part and disregarded the prison part.

Nan never concerned herself about her qualifications for jobs before she applied for them. She could dream, couldn't she? Other people played the lottery or spun the online dating roulette wheel; she applied for jobs.

She had to do something; she held the dubious distinction of treading water in her profession for twenty-five long years, still stuck on the entry-level librarian step on the civil service ladder in the Philadelphia public library system. People she'd graduated with from library school had risen over the years to become department heads, system managers, and directors. Not Nan. She disliked ambitious librarians clawing their way up. She had other priorities in life—so many women, so little time.

But now she was fifty years old, and what did she have to show for herself? A studio apartment so small she could lie on her lumpy futon, reach her arm out, and open the refrigerator door. A heart so bruised from disappointing love affairs that she was surprised it still worked to move blood around her body. A city full of reminders of the hopeful young Nan who had moved there to take her very first job after graduating from her Master of Library Science program. Her very first job that was still her only job; if it weren't so pathetic, it would be laughable.

The geographic cure for what ailed her life—that was the ticket. She craved distance from this city full of her mistakes, a clean landscape to start over in.

She didn't know why happiness was so hard for her to achieve. She felt that life rubbed her the wrong way, like when you put on an itchy sweater and you couldn't wait to rip it off. It wasn't depression; it wasn't melancholy; it was something else, something missing. She had a starved beast-child inside her, living on whatever crumbs of attention and affection she could find in the world; she hated knowing that about herself.

She wanted to be happy at unexpected times, to feel that her life was amazing, to enjoy little things like watching squirrels go crazy running up and down the trees into their hidey-holes, chasing one another and bouncing from branch to branch like acrobats.

If she got to that level of happy, she'd be the first woman in her family to do so, which would be quite an achievement among the martyrs, worriers, and sad sacks she came from. Time was running out; she was impatient, demanding herself to do something, anything, right now.

Wait, this job posting was different: Town Librarian, Pinetree, New Jersey.

She had never seen an ad like that before. A slow excited burn started in her stomach. Or was that acid building up from her liver, overworked by too much cheap wine chugged down too fast? The potato chips and onion dip she had for dinner probably didn't help either.

When Nan located Pinetree on a map of southern New Jersey, she saw a tiny dot surrounded by a national forest reserve. The details in the job posting were sparse, which was unusual, and the requirements were even more sparse—they asked only for an accredited Master of Library and Information Science degree, which Nan actually had. Although hers was an ancient, creaky version of the degree. She flinched at the listed salary, even less than the pitiful one she was making as Librarian I in the Philadelphia public library system. But that didn't matter. She was playing her job roulette game. It was all in good fun.

She poured herself another wallop of wine and applied for the job. Hope felt like that third glass of wine on a rainy night, a little luxury to warm herself by.

CHAPTER TWO

PINETREE, NEW JERSEY, could have been the setting for every movie set in an idyllic small town that Nan had ever seen, with a wide, walkable Main Street flanked by stately sycamore trees and stores people actually needed—grocer, liquor, barber shop, hardware, coffee shop, dry cleaner, bakery, furniture and antiques, pharmacy, and several delis—with an actual town clock looming over the scene. How cool was that?

Nan found the library easily, on the corner of Main Street and Central Avenue. The squat gray concrete building epitomized utilitarianism in a no-nonsense, no-frills square shape, with steep entry steps and a dented, faded book return drop box on the curb. Not very inviting. It clashed with the whole rest of Main Street, in fact.

She took a deep breath, pulled the heavy door open too fast, and smashed herself hard in the shoulder with it. *Do not react, swallow that searing pain. You do not want SHIT to be the first word these people hear from your mouth.*

Nan felt instantly at home, and she knew why. Although the library's exterior was not like the majestic Wilmington Public Library she had loved as a child growing up in Delaware, the inside summoned up all of the same delights as her hometown library. The smell of old books, that delicious mushroomy fragrance. The solid curve of a mahogany chair softened by decades of human rumps settling in for a long read. The pleasure, as intoxicating as a sexual thrill, of being surrounded by walls and walls of shelves packed tight with hardback books.

Nan breathed it all in and felt herself wanting this place to be hers. Her palms itched with the desire to touch everything, to mark this territory as her own.

Desire was not her friend though. Wanting brought disappointment; she had learned that the hard way.

The library board of trustees were gathered around a large mahogany table in the Reference Room. Pip (short for

Phillip, he announced, as if she cared) Conti, the fortyish board president who was also the superintendent of schools, was conducting the interview. He had a head as big as a moose's and carried himself like a former high school football star, cocking his head and pausing as if he heard applause every time he spoke. Nan disliked him immediately and intensely; she could recognize a blowhard a mile away.

She almost never got interviews for jobs she applied to, so she was quite rusty at the whole ask-me-a-question-and-I'll-answer-it-intelligently-and-persuasively-yet-charmingly bullshit. She limped her way through most of the interview, hating the sound of her own lame answers.

Valiantly, she tried to make substituting for the children's librarian once a year sound like she was indeed an accomplished storyteller and youth program organizer. She puffed up her required annual perfunctory technology training into a specialty in IT and all its mysterious manifestations. For budget preparation and finance management, she hauled out examples from her long-ago graduate school classes, throwing buzzwords around in the hopes of dazzling board members who knew even less than she did. Sweating profusely, she hoped her black turtleneck hid the flood.

"I will be frank with you," Pip said finally, jumping up to

pace around the table, pointing at Nan. "We need new blood. We need the latest and the greatest new ways. We need to be drop-kicked into the twenty-first century. We need you to convince us that you are up to the challenge." He sat down, arms folded, and waited.

Nan figured her competition for the job were recent library school graduates because who the hell else would work for the absurdly low salary? And if they were aiming for recent graduates, no wonder they hadn't put any experience requirement in the job posting. So he was using *new* to mean *young*. He was really asking if she was too old to do this job. An undulating pain shot up her fifty-year-old backbone in response.

This was so unfair. After all, she was clearly a cool librarian. She had an arty, jagged, super-short haircut, colored with streaks of turquoise and pink; she wore all black clothes and hefty Doc Martens boots. Apparently, none of that counted with Pip.

But he wasn't the only one on this board. There were six others staring at her. None of them were exactly in the springtime of life. Everyone except Pip looked to be well over fifty, and several looked over seventy. They each got a vote on her being hired too.

Nan had learned one thing in all her years at the bottom.

Often it paid to go around an obstacle rather than try to batter it down. She leaned forward, ignored Pip, made eye contact one by one with the other board members, and lowered her voice as if she were telling them a very important secret.

"New is all well and good. But as you all know, there is absolutely no substitute for experience." She felt as if she was bowling with one pin left standing at the end of the alley, and she had knocked it down with her last ball. She saw in their eyes that they yearned for someone their own age, someone they could connect with in the shorthand of shared understandings and vocabulary, someone who didn't make them feel old and stupid. Vote for me, she begged silently.

*

THE NEW TOWN Librarian. Nan was as unknown as the inside of a brand-new book, still smelling of fresh ink, its pages immaculate before readers dripped red wine on them or used a banana peel for a bookmark. She stood grinning in the doorway of her tiny office behind the library's checkout desk, enjoying the view and congratulating herself as she had daily since she'd started.

Sun streamed in the large old windows, beaming warmth and light on the scene, making the polished mahogany tables look inviting enough to kiss, dust motes dancing over the room like little fairies in the air.

She was at long last a library director, with no one to answer to. In one move, she had catapulted to the top of the library ladder. It was only a small-town public library in South Jersey, and she was the only professional librarian on staff, but it would do. She was running the show.

At that exact moment, the front door was flung open by two shortish figures dressed head to toe in camouflage attire, with ski masks pulled over their faces and hoodies covering their hair.

"FUCKINGASSHOLECOCKSUCKERS," they shouted into the room, then raced away.

Mona Pinto, the chief library assistant, dropped with a thud onto the floor, fainting like a movie murder victim.

Shaky Leonetti, a library regular who had been reading the *Wall Street Journal*, ran to the door and started bashing it with his cane as though he was thrashing the intruders.

Dunkan Grasso, the big man-child who was the assistant to the chief library assistant, emitted a long stream of screams as though he was being repeatedly stabbed with a jagged knife.

Nan felt as if someone had grabbed her by the shoulders and shaken her until her brain rattled against her skull. She was as shocked as the time she'd been on a first (and last) date with a surly dental hygienist named Taffy, and the woman had thrown a Bloody Mary at the wall and stormed out of the restaurant, apparently enraged at the slow service.

A minute passed as slowly as a chapter in a bad book. They all started to breathe again.

"SUCKMYCOCK," the intruders opened the door again to scream, then ran away screeching, their laughter lingering in the quiet.

Dunkan and Shaky turned to look at Nan, then down at Mona, who remained collapsed on the floor on her back. It was a pity she'd worn such a short skirt that day as her current posture gave any onlooker a clear view all the way up to her pink flowered panties.

Nan marched over to the door. This was the first test of her authority, and she was going to pass it with flying colors. She opened the door with one swift thrust.

Outside, everything that usually happened at the 3:00 p.m. dismissal time for the middle school across the street continued as normal. Yellow school buses lined up by the curb, children climbing aboard, cars halted by the buses' flashing lights. At the corner, crossing guards with hand-held stop signs escorted children across the street.

No thugs in ski masks were in sight. Nan didn't know what she'd expected—for them to wait on the corner so she could catch up with them?

"They're gone," she reported back to the people in the library, who stood expectantly staring at her. She knelt on the floor next to Mona but had no idea what to do for a downed chief assistant.

"Should I slap her?" Nan asked. No one answered.

Nan picked up Mona's hand and let it drop to the floor. The woman wasn't faking it; she really was out cold.

"Mona, Mona, wake up," Nan said. She felt foolish. One of the many, many things they didn't teach you in library school—how to revive a fallen comrade.

When Mona finally opened her eyes, she said, "No one ever did that when the *last* librarian was here," as if Nan had brought the shouting, cursing thugs with her from Philadelphia to unleash on the town.

"I'm calling the police," Nan said, jumping up.

She would show them she could handle anything. There was nothing she hadn't seen in her decades as a low-level librarian shuttling around to where she was needed in public library branches all over Philly, thinking of the time she'd gone outside to get fresh air when a drive-by shooting erupted outside the branch, a bullet ricocheting right at her as she dove for the ground. From then on, she did without fresh air.

Then there was the serial masturbator in another building, who would whip his tool out and go at it while people walked around him looking for a bestseller or a book on how to train their dog. Nan had to tell him herself to put that little thing away and get out as the security guard was invariably elsewhere when it happened. If she could handle that, she could handle this.

She'd have to call a door repair service too, she saw. Mr. Leonetti's cane had left shattered cracks over the whole lower half of the door. She made a mental note not to aggravate him for any reason. He was trigger-happy with that cane.

The police officer who answered the call was a tall beefy woman stuffed into her uniform, buttons straining against her belly, her belt strapped tight with a mixture of weapons and odd tools hanging from it like she was a combination assassin/home contractor. Holding a tiny notebook suitable for an elf, she made scratch marks in it that looked to Nan like the officer wasn't even trying to take notes, more *pretending* she was taking notes while actually doodling. This officer was dying for a juicy murder case or, at least, a violent assault and was not thrilled to be investigating dirty words shouted into a public library, Nan was sure.

The EMTs came too, with two ambulances and what looked like every single volunteer first responder the town had. Nan worried that a shoving match might break out soon over who got to work on Mona first as they all crowded around her. She was fully awake now and smiling helplessly up at them. Soon, she had six EMTs working on her various body parts; Nan counted.

"So what was damaged?" the police officer asked Nan.

"You mean did they break the door? No, they didn't break it."

"But it's cracked," the officer said.

"I did that," Shaky volunteered. "Sorry. I got a little carried away."

The officer shook her head. "So the *intruders* did no damage."

"They damaged our whole vibe here," Nan said. "Isn't that a charge, disturbing the peace?"

The officer sighed, scratched again ineffectually in her notebook. "What were the exact words they screamed?"

Nan started to say them out loud, but everyone was looking at her, making her feel like she was the one who had screamed the bad words.

"I'll write them all down for you." Nan herself swore all the time. She had no problem with cursing, but she felt she was bringing the words back to the library by repeating them out loud.

The officer read the words, then made a twitching motion with her lips.

You think this is funny? Nan fumed, wishing she could say it out loud. But she was still on probation. She had to tip-toe around for ninety days trying not to offend anyone until they made her a permanent town employee.

"No threats then. They did no damage, and they made no threats," the officer said.

"They totally disrupted us. They scared people in a public place. They made my assistant faint; she could have had a heart attack," Nan protested.

"But she didn't, did she?"

The chief EMT, her voice heavy with disappointment, spoke up to say that Mona was fine and didn't need to go to the emergency room.

"Did you recognize their voices?" the officer asked.

"I'm new in town," Nan said.

"They sounded like they were disguising their voices," Dunkan offered. "You know how football players do that grunting, screaming thing when they run at you?"

The way he described it made it clear to Nan that football players had run at Dunkan that same exact way. No wonder he liked hiding out in the library. He wouldn't have to see many of them in here.

"No," the officer said. "I don't know how they do that. Do they do that? I don't follow sports."

Talk about your non sequiturs.

"How many of them were there?" the officer asked.

"Ten," Mona said, as Nan said, "Two."

"It seemed like there were a lot of them," Mona said, sniffing.

"Two," Nan said. "I'm positive." That was about the only thing she was sure of.

The officer continued her lackluster scratching into her tiny notebook. This was ridiculous. Nan felt she was letting the officer down, like she should have been reporting a Molotov cocktail thrown into the library. Now *that* would have been worth the officer's time.

"So what are you going to do?" she demanded.

"Let me put it this way, if you could identify them, we might have a shot. But you can't, can you?"

"Is it my fault those punks dressed up like soldiers and

shouted like football players?"

"It's not your fault, ma'am." The officer stood up. "We'll do everything we possibly can."

Which is zero. After the officer left, the library staff and the people in the library all looked at Nan as if waiting for her to announce Plan B.

"I'll think of something," Nan said. The feeling of all eyes on her was intoxicating. She was the Town Librarian now, and she would fix everything.

CHAPTER THREE

NAN FLUNG OPEN her refrigerator, hoping to find anything edible inside. A piece of cheese, a bottle of Prosecco (that counted as nourishment), leftover anything, a jar of pickles even. It would have been a small miracle if any food had been there because she had not grocery shopped since she'd moved in. She was naked, finding her new apartment in Pine-tree to be way overheated; the temperature was controlled from downstairs where her landlords, Joe and Immaculata Fortunato, lived.

Why did they keep the heat turned up so very high? Maybe because Joe and Immaculata were as old as Rome.

Joe was a sweetheart—Nan could already tell—a short courtly guy with a shy smile and brown eyes that shone like a happy puppy's. But that Immaculata, she was a handful—she of the port-wine birthmark of raised bumps and ridges that covered half of her face, she of the sharp eyes and rounded body, she of the housedress du jour. Many of Immaculata's housedresses had a Florida theme for some reason, with over-sized grapefruits, lemons, and oranges adorning her large breasts and buttocks. Nan felt as if she was living in Immaculata's tropical paradise.

Every day when Nan got home, she took off her clothes and opened her windows for relief. No one could see her anyway, in this second-floor apartment on top of a farmhouse. All she could see were fields and woods from her windows, no one in nearby houses to spy on her.

She had jumped at the chance to rent the apartment after one of the board members suggested it, with its two bed-rooms, full bathroom, and its own outside entrance in the back on top of wooden stairs. After her studio apartment in Philly, it seemed immense, the whole top floor of a house. It was close enough to walk to work, on a quiet farm road a mile from the center of town, and was completely furnished. It was easy. All she had to do was move her clothes in.

The teal farmhouse reminded her of the dollhouse she'd shared with her sisters, with all those windows like wide-open eyes and the front porch with rockers that moved in the wind as if ghosts were sitting in them reading.

The furniture in her apartment cracked her up—the 1950s kitchenette with red vinyl chairs that made a little sigh when she sat on them; the blocky vintage TV in the living room, facing a black faux leather recliner that Nan despised the look of but lounged in every night with relief, her feet propped up and her head flung back; the disturbingly ornate white French provincial bedroom set with a bed so high Nan felt like she was trapped in "The Princess and the Pea" fairy tale when she climbed up on it.

She had abandoned her own furniture in Philadelphia. It had been the perfect time to ditch reminders of all the exes she'd acquired it with, forget all the times she'd moved with it in high hopes of one relationship or another lasting past six months. So this weird furniture mix would have to do for now.

The rent was very low, affordable with her tiny salary, and Immaculata even waived the security deposit because Nan was the Town Librarian and therefore constitutionally unable to be a bad tenant, evidently.

No matter how long she stared into the refrigerator, food

did not appear. She had forgotten to bring a sandwich home, dammit. She sighed, trying to imagine the effort of putting all her clothes back on and going to get takeout from one of the Italian delis where she'd been buying her lunches. No one delivered in this town, and she still couldn't wrap her brain around that.

The inner door that led from her kitchen down to the first floor rattled alarmingly. What the hell was that? Nan heard strange sounds, thumping bumping murmuring, boots tramping up and down. That must be Joe. He always wore work boots.

"Open up," Immaculata called out. "We got stuff for you."

"I'm naked," Nan shouted back, unnerved.

It sounded like Joe ran down the stairs.

"Nothing I haven't seen before." Immaculata laughed.

What had Nan gotten herself into here? She'd always lived in high-rise city apartments, with neighbors who kept their eyes down as they passed in the halls and ignored one another in the elevators.

"I'll wait," Immaculata said finally.

Nan stood frozen, unsure of what was worse, antagonizing her landlady who lived inches away or allowing this invasion of her privacy in what clearly would not be a one-time incursion.

She was ragingly hungry though. What if Immaculata was bringing food? She had often been tantalized by the smells wafting up from below. Nan pulled on shorts and her favorite T-shirt that read *Nobody Knows I'm a Lesbian* and let Immaculata in.

"Hold the door open," Immaculata ordered. With two hands, she delivered a huge jug of deep red wine. She put it under the table as if that was its designated place.

"Joe makes this," she said. "He don't even drink. It messes with his head, and that's not too good in the first place."

Suddenly Nan liked Immaculata a whole lot more. Homemade red wine often had an alcohol content that was double that of wine bought in liquor stores, and it had to taste way better than the cheap box wine that was all she could afford.

Then Immaculata lifted platters and bowls to the table, pointing out stuffed mushrooms, peppers and eggs, meatballs and ravioli, and an entire carrot cake. Had she forgotten Nan was living all by herself? This was enough food for a family of ten. But Immaculata wasn't done. She heaved bags full of what Nan thought of as ingredients—potatoes, broccoli crowns, tomatoes, cabbage, onions, and lemons. Nan didn't cook; what the hell was she going to do with this?

"We went to the market today, figured you could use a few things." Immaculata settled herself at the kitchen table without being asked. "Get some glasses out."

Nan opened cabinets until she found some, while Immaculata pretended she didn't know exactly where the glasses were. Of course, she did. Everything here was hers. Immaculata hoisted the jug up to pour Nan a big glass of wine and herself a shot-sized one.

I have no willpower against good food and wine. That's a fact. I'll deal with setting boundaries with Immaculata later.

Nan sat down and dug in, as eager as a pig to a trough.

"So who does your hair?" Immaculata rolled her eyes.

I take it you don't approve.

"Did your hairdresser get interrupted in the middle of working on you? She left one side shaved and one side long," Immaculata said.

"I love my hair. Everyone loves my hair." Nan wasn't happy about this turn in the conversation, but she didn't put her fork down. These were actual homemade ravioli.

"What's with all those crazy streaks? Was she using up

all her leftover colors or what? You got pink. You got green. You got purple." Immaculata laughed so hard her bosom bobbed up and down.

Could it be that Immaculata actually liked her? Was joking around her love language? Nan chose to respond with a friendly overture. She did not want to get on bad terms with a woman who had the power to make her life miserable, that was for sure.

"These meatballs are incredible," she said with her mouth full.

Immaculata nodded as if to say, *Of course they are; I made them.*

They sat companionably for a few minutes, Immaculata sipping her wine and Nan moaning over the stuffed mushrooms.

"So you read a lot? Aren't you worried your eyeballs will fall out from all that reading?" Immaculata asked.

"They do fall out once in a while. I just pop them right back in."

When Immaculata guffawed, Nan was so relieved. She wanted to keep the flow of this gorgeous food coming forever. She'd play nice to make that happen.

CHAPTER FOUR

NAN'S WORKDAY STARTED with Mona bursting into tears first thing in the morning and running into Nan's office to sob, chest heaving while blowing her nose and gasping as if she'd been attacked. Nan fought the impulse to lock Mona in the office and run away.

"What is it?" Nan asked. She had an outsized fear of cancer and hoped it wasn't that. She knew it wasn't true that cancer was contagious, but it kept getting closer and closer to her. The skull-making demon disease killed people before they died, leaving them walking around hairless, burned skeletons until it was a relief for everyone when they finally died. Both of her parents had died young of cancer, within a year of each other, when Nan was still a teenager. Even thinking the word made that spot in her right armpit twinge. *Is that where it will start in me?*

"I'm so ashamed. This never happened in my family before. I can't bring myself to say the words out loud," Mona said.

Then don't. I don't really care.

"You don't have to talk. Take a day off. You don't have to work when you're so upset," Nan said.

"I can't go home. He's there. My son."

"Your son who just got married?" Nan had overheard way too much about that wedding. She actually knew the color of the bridesmaids' dresses (periwinkle), the name of the maid of honor (Tabitha Teti), and how many people ordered the vegetarian option that the caterer insisted was necessary for the sit-down dinner (sixteen, which shocked Mona as she had no idea she even knew one vegetarian, let alone sixteen).

"Yes, he came back home," Mona sobbed.

"To visit?"

"No, he's getting a d... He's getting a d..."

Dog? He's getting a dog? What's so terrible about that?

"They dated all through high school. And college. Then

she went to pharmacy school. Then they got married. Now he says they're getting a d..." Mona said.

"Divorce? They're getting a divorce?" Nan asked. What a ridiculous guessing game this conversation was.

"I can't say the word. It's our first one in the family. We don't get di-i-i-vo-o-r-ced," Mona choked out.

Nan wondered if she'd been caught in a time warp, and she was now back in the 1950s. Was this town ringed by the Pine Barrens an enchanted village of the past?

"I'm sorry to hear that, Mona."

I'm sorry you need to spill your guts right when I'm trying to meet a 10:00 a.m. deadline to finalize my book order for the month.

"He said marriage wasn't what he thought it would be. That's all he'll say. What could that possibly mean?"

That marriage wasn't what he thought it would be, seems clear enough to me.

Mona laid her head down on Nan's desk. Her bouffant lacquered hair did not budge. What would it be like to have hair so hard that it held its shape in an emotional crisis?

Once again, Nan was shocked at what they hadn't taught her in library school. She didn't mean to be cold. She realized people's personal lives affected their work lives, but she really

really really really did not want to hear any more about Mona's son's marriage on the rocks.

She was a tiny bit curious though. Had the hapless couple been sleeping with each other since high school? Maybe the glow had worn off through their long engagement. Or had they held off on full intercourse till marriage and that was what caused the big disappointment when they finally did it? Straight people were so funny sometimes. Such high expectations for what could take time, practice, and alcohol to get right.

"I can't show my face in town. No one must know. The priest—what will the priest say? I feel like such a failure. My husband and I have been married for thirty-four years. What kind of example have we shown my son?" Mona picked her head up to wail.

"What else does your son say?"

"He says they both agree. It's a mutual breakup. She's not upset; he's not upset. Did you ever hear of such a thing?"

"Well, yes. It's not so unusual."

Trust me. I'm the queen of breakups. I've heard it all.

"I guess it's nobody's business why they broke up, right? That's their business, even if they are family," Nan added.

"I have to walk around this town and hear the whispers.

I have to face the gossip. The big wedding we threw them, three priests married them, everyone in town came to the reception. So many people danced at their wedding. All those presents still in their boxes. They didn't even write their thank-you notes yet. I feel so terrible."

"Is it your fault, Mona?" Nan put her hand on Mona's arm. She felt silly doing that but couldn't think of any other gesture to make except shaking the woman, and that wouldn't do. "Is it really your fault?"

Mona stared at her for a long time. "You're not from here. You have no idea what my life is like," she said finally. She stood up. "I'm going home. Don't tell anyone. I mean anyone."

The day went from bad to worse quickly. The *New York Times* had failed to arrive on their doorstep, causing the old men who gathered by the door at the 9:00 a.m. opening time to lose their minds. They stood by the front desk, refusing to take their usual seats in the reading room as if standing there breathing on Nan and Dunkan would make the newspaper appear.

Dulcie Mainwaring from Barbara Pym's *No Fond Return of Love* popped into Nan's mind. How Dulcie always found public libraries a bit upsetting because of all the odd characters one found there. There was an apt Barbara Pym observation for almost any situation in life, Nan found. That was precisely why she was Nan's all-time favorite British novelist. Nan believed she deserved bonus reader points because so many people didn't know her work. BP was her special little secret, the one author she could whip out whenever people asked who her favorite writer was.

"Where is it, when is it coming, did someone steal it?" the men asked Nan.

I don't know, and I can't make it materialize out of thin air, she wanted to say.

Instead, she asked Dunkan to take petty cash and go buy a copy from the drugstore. They weren't supposed to do that. They were supposed to get the delivery service to bring another one and report a missing issue. But when they did that, the paper didn't get there until the midafternoon or sometimes even the next day. Nan was afraid the old men would have a group seizure or heart attack right in the library if they had to wait that long. She'd never been around old people much until she got this job, never realized how welded they were to their daily routines.

Nan watched as Dunkan lumbered down the street. He was the most peculiar walker she'd ever seen, his body rocking side to side like a giant stuffed animal lurching along. She couldn't imagine how long it would take him to get anywhere that way. He had to catch his breath after every few steps. The wait for his return seemed endless. When he finally got back with the newspaper, he placed it on the front counter and stepped back.

The old men gathered around it, grabbing at the sections they wanted. It was a feeding frenzy, and they were the devouring sharks. Nan knew then she should have told Dunkan to buy several copies. She had to put her body in the middle of the fray, separate the sections on the front counter, insist "One at a time please," and stare down the men until they seemed a little bit ashamed of themselves, meekly taking a section and sitting down.

"I hate the health section. I don't want this crap," one of them muttered.

"I got education. Who the hell wants that?" another one said, slapping the paper with his palm.

It took Nan an hour to settle the men down, standing over them, glowering to let them know she wasn't going to put up with any more grabbiness or nasty remarks. Dunkan wouldn't do it. He was afraid of them, and it showed.

They did have weapons, Nan realized. Those canes were

no joke. She wouldn't put it past them to have knives in those canes that could pop out when they needed extra power. And they wouldn't get in trouble for wielding those weapons. All they had to say was it was a mistake, the cane slipped, they didn't mean it. Those old guys could get away with murder.

Then it was time for preschool story time. Nan was learning that three-to-five-year-olds were either charming delights or little jerks. There was no in-between. That day, they were little jerks. They were apparently bored by the story of small animals gathering underneath a mushroom that kept growing as the rain came down. Nan actually loved the story, but no matter how much her voice rose or how animated her gestures were, the children didn't care. They wouldn't take their eyes off the ringleader—that Angelica who cockily took off her socks and shoes, and then everyone took off their socks and shoes, then Angelica threw herself down flat on her back and rolled around like a drunken yogi, and they all rolled around like drunken yogis.

Nan was exhausted by the time story time was over. She had a blinding headache between her eyebrows, probably an aneurysm getting ready to explode in there. She limply waved goodbye to the children and their caregivers and sagged in the rocking chair.

The bad day ended worse than she could ever have imagined when she went downstairs to the Children's Room and smelled a horrible odor near the new picture book shelves, where the most beautiful books with gorgeous shiny illustrations were. These were the ones newly arrived and still fresh before grubby preschoolers with their dirty little fingers smeared the pages and tore them in their haste to swallow the book whole and before snot and vomit landed inside. Someone or several someones, judging by the volume of the liquid, had peed all over the new picture books, splashing urine all over the books, the shelves, and the carpet.

Nan gasped. Who would do such a thing? Was it the obscenity-screaming thugs again? Why? What had she ever done to deserve this? And most importantly of all, why did the library not budget for a full-time custodian? Because she couldn't ask the assistants to clean this up. That was not an option. The one principle she ran her work life on—formed from working shitty part-time jobs with awful bosses before and during graduate school—was never ask anyone to do anything you wouldn't do yourself.

So she breathed through her mouth as she found a broom, garbage bag, and rubber gloves, as she swept the books clumsily into the trash, as she wrote down their titles so she could replace them, as she sopped up the urine with paper towels, as she threw up into the wastebasket.

When Dunkan clomped down the stairs to see what was taking her so long, she teared up as she waved him away, then she let a few tears out as he found more rubber gloves and helped her. She finally went upstairs, leaving the bag downstairs as evidence. This was public property damage; she would have to document the vandalism with another police report.

She held her tears firmly inside when the officers came, different ones this time. They knocked on the locked library door as gingerly as if they were making a visit to tell a family that their loved one had died in a car accident or by suicide down by the town lake.

No, there were no cameras in the Children's Room. She answered their questions mournfully, knowing that there was nothing they could do. No one had seen anyone go downstairs except the usual after-school crowds and then parents with their kids after dinner loading up on bedtime stories and books to help with homework. She and Dunkan and their student worker Amo Gonzalez—who, although he never took his earbuds out and seemed to pay no attention to anything but the music in his ears, had a perfect shelving record, had never missed a Dewey decimal point carried out to its furthest point—had not seen a thing as they came and went from the Children's Room. No one had reported anything. The vandals must have seized a moment at the end, when the room was briefly empty, when the staff was busy elsewhere, and then they'd emptied their bladders on the most pristine new books.

"All we can say is it must have been a boy or boys," the first officer whispered as if told one must always be quiet in a library even when investigating a crime after hours. "Because no way could a girl have climbed up there and let go. The angle's all wrong."

Nan pictured a girl standing on top of the bookshelf and pulling down her pants, squatting and peeing like a camper in the woods. She started to laugh then, heard the hysteria in her voice, that awful word still used against women, but she *was* hysterical; she couldn't help it, couldn't stop laughing.

"I'm sorry, I'm sorry. It's been a long crazy day," she finally choked out.

The officers left shaking their heads, and the day was finally over.

CHAPTER FIVE

SHE SMELLED RUSSO'S Deli before she saw it. She had walked past it several times before without going in, but now the front door was propped open, and the amazing scents of sharp provolone, roasted garlic, and multiple unidentified other temptations propelled her inside.

"Hey, beautiful." A bare-armed woman with the cutest butchy haircut called out over the microphone at the deli counter as if she were announcing the next customer's lunch-meat order was ready.

Nan looked around. Who was she talking to?

"Yeah, you, babe," the woman said, grinning. Every

single thing about her made Nan's gaydar ring out as if a crazed bell choir was in full concert mode inside her.

The deli was full of women pushing small shopping carts. Were men even allowed in here? It didn't look it. The women all swiveled around, laughing at Nan. She didn't know how to respond to teasing. Her family didn't tease; her lovers didn't tease; her friends didn't tease. She couldn't even remember the last time someone teased her like this, maybe in high school?

"That's Thomasina, they call her T," one of the older women leaned over to tell Nan. "She owns the place."

T came out from behind the counter holding a long, thick salami. She chased the ladies around with the salami strategically placed at her crotch, making them all crash their carts into one another, laughing and slapping back at her.

Nan snorted and stepped back. This T woman had apparently never heard of sexual harassment (even though she looked to be thirty-something and should know better; surely, she'd had to watch that HR training at least once in her work life).

"You're the new librarian, right? Philly girl." T poked her salami at Nan's belly.

Nan had been the cover story in the town's newspaper

that week with the regrettable headline written by their college intern: *Pink Hair, Don't Care: Meet Our New Town Librarian.* So she guessed her tiny flame of fame was to be expected. She nodded.

"Hey, librarian, what you got in your backpack, a bunch of books? You should knock off all that reading. Your brain is going to explode. Then I'll have to clean that up all over my store—cleanup in aisle four, hahaha." T was obviously still performing for her customers, her voice loud enough for every single shopper to hear.

If she wasn't so adorable, I'd hate her anti-reading guts. But that muscly body packed into those tight jeans, those tanned chiseled arms, those eyes as warm as melted chocolate, that mouth as wide as... That's enough of that.

"I won't explode in here." That was the best Nan could come up with.

T leaned close to whisper in Nan's ear. "You explode wherever you want, beautiful."

After she steadied her knees by leaning against a tower of boxed pasta in every size and shape imaginable, Nan walked out clutching a warm filone (which she had just discovered was an Italian baguette) like a sword in her hand.

Stand back, deli flirt.

She had no business messing around with women and distracting herself until she was off probation. Three long months. Make that two and a half for time already served, but who was counting?

CHAPTER SIX

IT WAS 3:00 P.M., so Nan took up her post by the front door as if she were the official library greeter. She felt ridiculous standing there, but she was so worried the obscene thugs would come back, and Pip Conti would blame her. The library board meeting was coming up. She could picture the first two agenda items:

1. Police called to library for obscene intruders.

2. Police called to library for urinary vandalism.

If she didn't get this library under control, she'd be dismissed during her ninety-day probation period and labeled for life as an unworthy librarian.

She'd applied for a million jobs before, and this was the one and only offer she had gotten, so how the hell would she support herself if she lost this job? Going back to her old Librarian I job was not an option as the Philly library system was in a hiring freeze again. That door was firmly shut. Even if there were openings, she wasn't confident they'd hire her back again. Thinking of her lackluster performance ratings and her evident indifference, she admitted they could do better than her. She had to make this new job work, end of story.

The thugs were from the middle school across the street from the library; she was sure. Her two clues: they were shortish, and they appeared right after school let out.

That school was full of beasts—children at that horrible age when puberty hit some but not all; when some sprouted up as tall as adults and were in the same classes as others who still looked like children; when some turned into comedians with the sharpest wit and an eye for absurdity and others turned into surly beings who thrashed their way through life, ripping branches off trees and stomping on flower beds for fun, littering their way across town.

Nan didn't actually know what she'd do if the door was flung open by those punks in ski masks again. Yell obscenities back at them? Shove them out and pull the door shut? It had all happened so fast before. Nan, the staff, and library users had all frozen in place, not able to do anything to stop them quickly enough. She was sure that was part of the fun for the thugs.

At 3:10 p.m., Mona called out, "The state arts council is on the phone for you."

Nan was excited. This must be about the grant proposal she had sent them for a groundbreaking (well, for Pinetree it was) lunchtime classic books lecture series. The series would focus on those hard, fat books everyone always meant to read but never did. She envisioned fascinating conversations led by lively academic experts, their speaker fees fully paid by the arts council. Maybe they would bring amazing visual aids— gory relics like the bones and teeth of saints for Chaucer's *The Canterbury Tales*, for example. If Pip Conti wanted new, Pip Conti would get new.

"Our town is so ready for a cultural program like this," Nan began. "People are desperate for intelligent conversations and to be around smart people."

BAM, the front door was flung open.

"FUCKYOUMOTHERFUCKERS," the thugs screamed.

"What was that?" the arts coordinator asked.

"I'll have to call you back," Nan said, hanging up and

running to the door. But it was too late. Too late for the arts council program probably too.

"Did you see anything?" Nan shouted to the staff.

Dunkan was holding on to the desk like it was a life raft. "Face. Covered. Mask. Hood," he panted.

"God DAMN it," Mona shouted from the lap of Shaky Leonetti, who had caught her when she fell backward. He was smiling, as delighted as a puppy that had just caught a hot dog rolling off a paper plate at a picnic.

"I'm going to get to the bottom of this," Nan said. "Don't you worry about that. I swear they will not be bothering us anymore. That was the last time."

She had no idea on earth what to do. But she was not going to let those punks win.

*

EVERY STEP OF her walk home hurt Nan. Her body played out her worries in the flesh. Her head throbbed in tune to the funeral dirge playing in her mind if she lost this job. A muscle in her right buttock kept spasming, forcing her to stop and shake out her leg repeatedly like a fox with its foot in a trap. Even her teeth hurt with each breath she sucked in. On top of everything else, did she have a dental infection that would spread to invade her heart muscle and kill her?

Immaculata was in the backyard waiting for her. Nan wanted to snarl at her. But she held a jug of Joe's amazing wine, and Nan was out of wine.

"Thank you very much." Nan held out her arm to accept the wine.

Immaculata held firmly to the jug. "I'll bring it up."

So the price I pay for the wine is you, Immaculata. You at my kitchen table. You talking to me when all I want to do is be left alone.

An hour later, Nan felt quite wonderful. The wine was so powerful. She wanted to throw her head back and laugh BWAHAHA, like an anemic vampire chugging down whole blood. God, where did that come from? She hated vampire novels.

The study of odd couples was one of Nan's favorite mental hobbies. She rarely heard Joe say more than two words at a time, while Immaculata talked enough for both of them. He was so older-Italian-movie-star-handsome, and she was quite peculiar-looking. Joe was a softie, and Immaculata was a bulldozer of the highest order. Joe was constantly in motion; he walked all over town all night long after everyone else was asleep. "Because he's not right in the head" was how

Immaculata had put it. She herself rarely left the house. How in the world had they gotten together and stayed together? Nan finally asked Immaculata.

"That Joe. He's in love with this town. Always has been. Everyone knows. If he could of married a town, he would of." Immaculata laughed, her mouth wide open, square little teeth flashing against her purple skin.

"But he fell in love with you instead."

"I don't know about all that. He had to marry me."

"What do you mean?" Nan didn't really care about the story, but she cared about this wine. It was smoothing out all the sharp edges. She slouched back in her chair.

"My dad asked him to marry me. And he was Joe's boss, so Joe had to."

"What, like a matchmaker?" Nan asked. Immaculata clearly enjoyed telling this story; Nan was intrigued.

"My dad, Sammy the tailor, had to pay somebody to marry me because of my face. He gave Joe a lot of money, plus he bought us this house."

Am I supposed to pretend that massive maroon birthmark splitting her face in half is hardly noticeable? Nan gave a *hmmm* in response, her fallback all-purpose noncommittal sound.

"Well, nobody else wanted to wake up looking at this every morning," Immaculata said. "Joke was on him. He could have saved his money. Joe would have done anything for my dad, anything for anybody in this town. He's simple like that."

"You don't care?" Nan couldn't help putting herself in Immaculata's place. How would she feel about climbing into bed every night with someone who had been forced into marrying her to keep her job? She thought that bed would be a chilly place. But then again, once a love affair went sour, in those excruciating last few months before a breakup, nothing could top that for the horrible soul-crushing pain when your lover turned away from you night after night, when she refused to say what was wrong, when she came up with excuses to avoid touching you. Nan had been there many times.

"Who cares? I got what I want," Immaculata said. "A house of my own. Got away from my family. The hell with all them. They leave me alone over here."

"How'd you make that happen? Maybe I'll try it on my sisters." Nan had been working herself up to call Franny and Regina. She'd never thought about ditching them altogether like Immaculata had though.

"I told them don't bother us. Me and Joe are good on

our own."

What in the world did Joe and Immaculata see in each other? It was a mystery. But surely, liking the same things for dinner was one of the best predictors of a long and happy marriage, as Dr. Parnell proclaimed in Barbara Pym's *Some Tame Gazelle.* That was not actually easy to pull off in real life. Nan recalled all the food fights in her relationships. This one didn't eat whey (Nan still had no idea where whey appeared in food or how to avoid it), that one ate only pea protein, the last one served disgusting gas station hotdogs for dinner.

The wine was beginning to work hard on Nan. She couldn't remember the last time she'd sat around like this, drinking and talking with someone she hardly knew.

A sharp pain pierced her neck. *Is that where my thyroid is? Does red wine aggravate the thyroid? How long does it take to die when the thyroid stops working?*

Stop thinking about my thyroid.

Immaculata patted herself on the cheek as if she'd forgotten about her birthmark and was checking to see if it was still there.

"Do you ever think about getting it removed?" Nan wondered what she would look like without it.

"Joe thinks if I get it taken off, my brains will fall out." Immaculata laughed, shaking her head.

"We wouldn't want that."

"Maybe I'm cursed; what do I care?" Immaculata seemed to find being cursed a highly amusing fate.

Am I cursed? Are thugs and urinating vandals my inevitable fate? Will I be driven out of this town, thrown out of my job? Am I doomed to fail because I dared to shoot for more in my life? Nan was sliding down the slope of an alcohol buzz, heading for the vale of despair.

"I don't believe in curses," Nan declared as much to herself as to Immaculata. She resolved to find an answer for her work problems. After all, there was no one to kick them upstairs to. She was the boss now.

CHAPTER SEVEN

NAN DREADED HER first library board of trustees meeting, but the night came anyway. Pip Conti sat at the head of the table, of course. Since she'd started work, Nan had learned a bit about some of the others. Chuck Hornfeck was the hardware store owner with a PhD in philosophy—his degree was just for fun, he'd said; Nan loved him immediately. Sissy Saccomanni ran the town's travel agency, was the wife of a town councilman, and was known for her extensive Scarves of the World collection. Paul Puddu was first cousin of the mayor and seemed to be crazy about his wife; he brought her up all the time, an endearing trait to Nan. The rest were assorted town residents (Toni Ann Baez, Martin Feliciano, Nefertiti Button), who simply cared about the library enough to agree to serve on the board.

Nan sat quietly while the board attended to their usual business of approving minutes, reviewing bills and expenditures, and setting a timeline for the budget to be submitted to the town council and the state library. She would have to make a budget for the very first time in her life. The terror of it all. She'd become a librarian because she loved books and libraries; what the hell did money have to do with any of that?

The night before, Nan had lain awake preparing what to say about the police reports. Should she bring them up? What would she say if they brought them up? The fact was that *she* was the one running the building, not the board. She was supposed to manage everything. The word *manager* had tormented her in the dark. How could she possibly manage a library all by herself when she couldn't even manage her own life?

When the time for her report came, Nan struggled to sound calm and confident. She'd prepared a few remarks about her grant application to the state arts council, but she noticed them all clicking off when she started. They were clearly not interested in hearing about that as it was only a vague possibility at this stage, not a done deal.

Her right eye began to twitch so badly she could hardly see out of it.

"I understand you've been calling the police a lot," Pip Conti said, interrupting her. "What's the story?"

Nan's face grew hot. She made eye contact with Chuck Hornfeck, who smiled encouragingly at her. Sissy Saccomanni patted her lap under the table. Nan took a deep breath. She felt a rush of love for them.

You gave me a chance. I won't let you down.

"No story," she said firmly. "We had a few minor incidents. I feel it's best to work closely with our library liaison officer, don't you? Hand in hand, we'll smooth out any little troubles that come up." She pictured holding hands with the beefy female officer and nearly laughed out loud.

Pip Conti scowled and closed his folder.

"I adore the new book displays." Toni Ann Baez pointed to the front counter and nearby tables.

Bless you a thousand times for changing the subject.

Nan believed in book displays. Too many books crammed together on the shelves intimidated people. So she'd pulled books out and stood them up all over the place, with splashy colorful signs she made herself:

Books with Stupid Endings

Books the Library Shouldn't Have Bought

Books You Can Live Without

Books with Red-haired People in Them

Books Where Evil is Rewarded

Books Where it Rains All the Time

Books to Read When You Are Mad at the World

Books Nobody Wants to Read

"My wife told me about them," Paul Puddu said. "She thought they were a riot."

Martin Feliciano hopped up and leaned over Books Nobody Wants to Read.

"Girl, you're a little loopy, aren't you?" Nefertiti Button elbowed her playfully. She picked up two books from the Books Where Evil is Rewarded pile to check out.

"Yes, I am, thank you for noticing." When they all chuckled at Nan's joke—even Pip the Moosehead—she could breathe again. Her eye stopped twitching. She had a reprieve and another month to get through before her elevation to the throne of Town Librarian.

*

AFTER THE BOARD members left, Nan stayed behind to

pull out the files on previous library budgets, to get a head start on the baffling project. She had no idea on earth how to write a budget, let alone present one to the town council. Did it involve a Big Reveal, whisking a cover off a blown-up budget on an easel? What was the appropriate soundtrack? Should she practice an announcer voice (*And now, for your viewing pleasure, I present to you THE LIBRARY BUDGET, TA DA*)?

She did not want to do any of this hard stuff, she only wanted to do the fun librarian stuff—buying shiny new books, setting up cool displays, thinking up innovative programs that would be so popular people would line up around the block to get in.

There was no escaping the budget though. She had to produce one very soon, and she might as well get started. But she was so incredibly tired from her sleepless night and this long day full of troubles to get through.

I'm just going to rest my eyes for a minute, that's all.

She woke up to the sound of banging on the front door. Joe was out there, waving his hands at her. She unlocked the door and let him in.

"You didn't come home," he said.

This lovely man. No one had looked after her for a

thousand years, it seemed. Her dad had died before her wild years when she stayed out late and drank vodka in cars with bad girls.

"I came to get you." He crooked his elbow for her to hold on to in an old-fashioned gentlemanly manner as they descended the front steps. Her heart swelled at his sweetness.

They walked slowly down Main Street, Joe stopping occasionally to pick up a piece of litter or to try a shop door making sure it was locked. This was an old familiar routine, Nan recognized. At night, Joe owned this town.

He stopped in front of a mani-pedi salon, pointed to it. "Sammy's Tailor Shop. Used to be right there."

Nan remembered Sammy had been Immaculata's father and Joe's boss.

"Did you like working there?" she asked.

Joe laughed, a high-pitched giggle that surprised Nan. "That guy. He could talk your ear off. One-for-two sale. Go in for one suit, end up with two."

"Was he a good boss?"

"He picked me." Joe looked so proud. "I had nobody. Sixteen, all my relatives gone. I slept in the back room. He taught me. I was a good tailor."

Nan wished she could say she was a good librarian. Not

quite yet, but maybe someday. It must be wonderful to feel proud of yourself when you got old, to look back on your work like it meant something.

Joe pointed to a house that reminded her of an over-stuffed chair, objects spilling out from inside to the wide porch and driveway. "Stumpy."

"The house is stumpy?"

He laughed again. "Stumpy Locatore lives there. My friend. He has this red barn on his blueberry farm. All us old guys go there to eat when the sun comes up. We call it the café. He makes the best pepper and egg sandwiches. Oh boy."

This man is living a beautiful life. This man is happy.

"You like dogs?" Joe asked.

Nan nodded. They had reached the street's far end, where the big houses with gated lush front yards were. To her astonishment, on both sides of the street, dogs were waiting by their gates. They wagged their tails and grinned at Joe. None of them barked; they knew to stay silent. One by one, Joe unlocked their gates and let them out. Big hairy mutts, Rottweilers, beagle hunting dogs, German shepherds, little terriers, they all trotted alongside. They were a pack, and Joe was the leader. Nan felt like royalty.

Joe and the dogs walked her home and waited until she

went in and closed the door. He and the pack disappeared into the night, headed toward the town lake. All she heard was the wind in the trees and the jangling of the dogs' collars as they trotted away, flanking Joe like an honor guard.

She was home safe. That was a funny word for her to think of, *home*. She hadn't felt at home anywhere in the world for a very long time.

CHAPTER EIGHT

THE DELI FLIRT showed up at the door to Nan's office. "Hey, Philly, I came to see you. Show me around, why don't you?"

Nan wanted to say *Don't call me Philly*, but the truth was she loved bearing the city on her shoulders, carrying its name as her own. It made her feel special. At the moment, though, Philly seemed as far away as Reykjavik.

"Why, if it isn't Thomasina," Nan said.

"Oh god, don't call me that. You know I go by T."

Nan felt a jolt of pure joy to see her there.

"My spacious office, how do you like it?" she said. "You

could get lost in here." She waved her arm around her tiny office, big enough only for a desk and a narrow cabinet. It was a cubbyhole, really, with a curved bow window from where she could almost see Main Street if she stuck her head out and craned all the way to the right.

"Pretty sweet. What else you got?"

Nan walked her around the library, showing her everything she was proudest of: new shelving to highlight the new books because she wanted them to be the first thing people saw when they came in, to dispel the notion that this place was full of old books (which it mainly was, but she was going to do something about that the minute she got off probation); the row of sleek new computers tucked into a front corner; the laptops that could be checked out like books; the reading area with magazines and newspapers, fully occupied at the moment, Nan was proud to see.

This was strange though. There it was again. A book with the title *Help Me*—a psychological thriller with a cover showing a woman holding on as she dangled off a skyscraper—sat propped up in the middle of a table in the Reference Room. It didn't belong there, far from the fiction aisles. It was the third time this week that exact book had been carefully placed there. Nan put it back on the book cart to be reshelved yet again.

They went downstairs into the Children's Room with its brand-new beanbag chairs on the floor and freshly painted persimmon and purple walls. It also held the remains of a jail cell, with bars over small windows high in the wall, left over from when the building had housed the town jail.

It was a strange arrangement, having the Children's Room in the former jail, in a basement with narrow stairs down to it from the main floor, but they'd added a ramp to the downstairs entrance for people with strollers. It made the whole building accessible for wheelchairs, too, with a small elevator (available only for people with disabilities, of course, for fear of what a crowd of rowdy kids could do to it) to the main floor and mezzanine. *Allegedly* accessible was a more accurate description of the building; half the time the stinking elevator was out of order and waiting for service.

When they walked into the Children's Room, she saw an adult hardcover book, this one a memoir entitled *Save Me*, propped up on one of the tiny tables near the picture books for preschoolers. Next to it, face front to show the cover, another adult thriller showed a woman underwater, entitled *I'm Drowning*. Nan's head started to pound. Was someone trying to tell her something?

"Wow, you did good. This used to be so boring-looking in here," T said.

Nan decided to ignore the message books for now. "You remember?"

"Yeah, we used to have to come here after school all the time, me and my brothers. My mom thought we'd do our homework better if we were surrounded by books." T sat down at a child-sized table, barely fitting into the tiny chair.

"Did that work?"

"Sure. I was good in school. I like homework; it's like work. I like work. My brothers used to threaten they'd lock me in the jail cell if I didn't behave. They were beasts." T smiled, standing up. "Still are."

"I have a problem with beasts," Nan said. "Somebody peed on a bunch of brand-new books."

"Ewww, that's as nasty as it gets. We never did anything as bad as that."

"And these kids keep running over after school and screaming obscenities into the building and then getting away before we can catch them. The cops aren't doing a thing about it. It's driving me crazy."

"Lock the door and stand out there like a doorman for a while. They'll stop. You can let people in one at a time."

"I think that's against the fire code," Nan said. "You can't lock a door while people are inside."

"Stand out there on the steps then. That will send those beasts away."

"I'd feel ridiculous," Nan said. "I'm not a security guard. I have a master's degree."

"Make one of the others do it then."

"I never ask my staff to do things I wouldn't do myself."

"Rock and a hard place. You'll figure it out; you're a smarty pants," T said.

"Why, yes, I am."

"The smarter the pants, the harder they fall," T said.

Oh, god, help me keep my mind off that image. I have a library to whip into shape.

*

NAN STOOD BY the front door for a week as the middle school bell rang for dismissal. She felt like a fool. Nothing happened. Groups of students walked over; nobody screamed; nobody ran. They sat around the bigger tables, doing homework, laughing, talking in waves louder and then softer when Dunkan walked by. As if that guy would shush them. He was incapable of any kind of confrontation.

The very day Nan stopped waiting by the front door, the beasts returned as if they psychically knew she wasn't there. They screamed the worst obscenities yet, as though they'd been studying up on words during the week when she had waited by the door so they could return with a vengeance. They were the words Nan really hated—the sick words, the words used by haters.

Nan had to make another police complaint, even if they wouldn't do anything. She had to at least document it, to have an answer to the question of what she had done about the trouble, too big to ignore. "Can you please send the library liaison officer over again? We have to do something about this. It's getting worse."

The officer came with her little notebook, said the same things she'd said before, offered no real hope of a solution.

"Do you think they're the same kids who peed on our children's books?" Nan asked. Another question she never could have imagined having to utter in her professional life.

The officer shrugged. "No idea."

"Can't you investigate? Pay a snitch? Go undercover?" Nan's throat hurt when she spoke up, as though she had been screaming for hours. Which was exactly what she felt like doing.

"That's kind of TV stuff, not real-life policing."

"This isn't acceptable. You're supposed to do something. Not just write reports." Nan decided there was a fierceness in being this old—a take-no-prisoners feeling. She'd never before felt so powerful in her rage. If the police had no solutions for her, she'd damn well make her own and not feel bad about it.

"We're doing everything we can, ma'am," the officer said.

You're doing absolutely nothing. It's all on me.

The next day, before the middle school bell rang, Nan hid in the bushes—overgrown, thanks to the negligence of the town's road crew, who didn't see bush trimming as one of their imperatives when there were potholes and knocked-down stop signs to fix.

She held two fat red tomatoes, one in each hand. Courtesy of Immaculata's produce delivery to her apartment; she'd finally found a use for it instead of bringing it in to work to give away.

Two more tomatoes were on the ground, her backups. She was definitely right-hand dominant, so she planned to throw with her right hand and then shift the left tomato to the right quickly for the next throw. It was split-second timing, so she'd probably hit the door and the steps before she hit the bad kids, but she had to try something. She hadn't told the assistants what she was doing; she'd said she was taking a coffee break.

When she heard the pounding sound of running feet on the sidewalk and the HUH HUH HUH grunting, she stood up and aimed, throwing the tomato as hard as she could, yelling like a shot putter, "YAAAA."

One tomato landed on the side of one head with a satisfying *smack*, sending red pulp and seeds down in a shower. The other tomato landed on another kid's buttocks as they turned and ran. Nan jumped up and down, cheering for herself. Two dead-on hits on target, and she hadn't even practiced. She thought about chasing them, but the point was not to catch them. The point was that they'd have to explain their tomato stains to their parents or wash them themselves in secret. The point was that they'd have to rethink how exciting it was to torment the library.

It was tremendously fun to throw ripe tomatoes; she had no idea what a high that would give her. She was so happy she could have turned cartwheels on the library lawn if she still knew how to. She wanted to throw open the door and yell *Drinks for everyone, on me.* She wanted to turn on loud music and dance up and down the library aisles.

The door opened, and the assistants peeped out. To-mato juice and seeds were everywhere. Quickly, they brought out a mop and bucket of soapy water.

"What happened?" they asked.

Nan considered telling all, doing a victory dance right in front of the checkout desk. But an adult throwing tomatoes at children probably constituted assault or some criminal of-fense, so she simply smiled and said nothing. It was a big smile, though, a smile that lasted through the rest of the day and into the night.

"I'm proud of you, you badass superstar of a librarian," she said out loud into the mirror that night, making ridiculous toothy faces at herself.

*

SHE HID IN the bushes the next three days, loaded with to-matoes, and no bad children came. Then came a day of tor-rential downpour. She woke up knowing instinctively that they would be back that day, the little jerkoffs. But they couldn't outsmart her.

She borrowed a long yellow mackintosh from Joe, the kind farmers used when they had to go out in the rain to take care of animals. It had a huge, brimmed hood and fell all the way to her ankles. She was a priestess in it, holy and untouchable.

Before the middle school bell rang, she crouched behind the bush, on the opposite side from where she'd crouched the time before. She visualized her throws over and over in her mind, smashing the children right in their face masks. She tended to her anger like a bubbling pot on a stove, keeping it at the exact peak where boiling rage would make her aim perfect.

She heard the unmistakable sound of running. They had their masks pulled up, hoodies over their heads, exactly as before. One for each of you, she plotted as she tightened her grip on the tomatoes. And what perfect throwing tomatoes they were too. They fit exactly in her palms, so ripe that the smash would be spectacular.

BAM, she threw the first tomato just as the kid put their hand on the door, hitting their right ear. The kid fell over in surprise, slipping on the wet steps, howling like a toddler who'd dropped their ice cream, and landing on their ass on the pavement. *BAM,* she threw the next tomato at the second thug a little lower, hitting the kid right in the crotch, making them curl up into a ball on the steps and cry in pain.

She stood over them, bellowing, "You had enough? You

done now? Want the cops to call your parents to pick you up from jail?" She lowered her voice to sound as menacing as theirs. She reached toward them to pull down their masks, but they rolled away from her, got up, and tore down the street, not looking back.

The door opened a crack. There she stood, in her ridiculous long macintosh.

Mona said, "We made fresh coffee."

"I can't talk about it," Nan whispered as she shed her wet coat inside the door. "I'll get in trouble. I'm still on probation."

"Can't talk about what?" Mona said, winking. "I don't know what on earth you mean."

Nan relaxed, smiled, and realized how stiff she was from crouching, how tense her arms had been, waiting.

"Tell you what though," Mona said. "We all decided we have a craving for tomato sandwiches for dinner."

"Sounds perfect," Nan said. "Enjoy."

The *thwack* of the tomatoes landing replayed in her ears for hours, as enjoyable as a favorite song. Could she get away with this unorthodox remedy? At the moment, she didn't even care if it drove away the kids for good. She cared only about the jolt of confidence it gave her. What an unfamiliar, amazingly wonderful sensation. She wanted more, more, more.

*

NAN CALLED FRANNY, her oldest sister, first. It was so fun to rattle her.

"You'll never believe what I just did. These kids were harassing us at the library, and I chased them away by hurling tomatoes at them. It was a blast."

"That's assault with a…" Franny started in. She watched a lot of true crime shows and believed real life was extremely perilous as a result.

"With a what? Not-so-deadly weapon?"

"Assault *and* battery," Franny said. "They are going to put you in jail and throw away the key."

"Let them try and prove it." Nan enjoyed portraying herself as much braver and tougher than she actually was.

"I hope no one got really hurt. You know, an object can hit someone in just the right spot and disable them for life. I saw a show where a hard-boiled egg, thrown recklessly, took a man's EYE out." Franny was full of dire stories with horrible outcomes.

Talking to her sisters was both nerve-wracking and

annoying at the very same time; it took girding of Nan's loins.

Bad nerves were their birthright from a mother who shook and cried. She didn't *only* do those things. She also read them fairy tales and poems and took them to libraries, art museums, and parks. But mostly what stays with children are the fears and tears of their parents. Nan had been paralyzed when her mother cried.

"Why is Mom crying?" Nan had finally gotten up her nerve to ask her father when she was very young, so young she didn't know how bad it was to say that out loud. He wouldn't look her in the eyes but shook his head no at her. What did that mean? No, Mom wasn't crying? He didn't know why she was crying? It definitely meant she should go away and not ask again. Nan never did. Instead, she became a vigilant watcher of her mother.

Regina and Franny had taken their mother's crying even worse than she had. They'd grown up into nervous wrecks of women, queens of the worst-case scenario. They wouldn't let their children ride bicycles or play sports for fear of broken legs and concussions. They rarely left the tiny state of Delaware, where every part of it was familiar to them. Mostly they obsessed about the latest calamity in the news. And neither of them drank, which, in Nan's mind, was a crazy way to live.

Drinking was good for bad nerves. It calmed the jangling right the hell down. Nan never cried or got depressed when she drank; she was always happy and relaxed. She knew so many people who were on antidepressants and antianxiety medications for their nerves, but she'd rather drink. They were always having to get their medication adjusted anyway, sweating profusely, not able to have orgasms, not able to sleep, or not able to wake up. Or it would stop working altogether, and then their doctor would add new ones on top of the others to see what would happen, as if their bodies were nothing but a chemical experiment.

Nan wound Franny up as much as she could before letting her off the hook and calling Regina. Her specialty in worrying was medical issues, so Nan always started off with a list of her own current symptoms.

"My right eye has been twitching so bad. What do you think that could be?"

"Alcohol abuse," Regina said. "That's the top cause of eye twitching. How much have you been drinking lately?"

Not nearly enough.

Regina rattled off other possible causes of eye twitch: bright lights, too much screen time, stress, caffeine. How in the world she knew so much to worry about, right off the top of her head, was a mystery; Nan always had to look up symptoms in medical books.

People always think librarians know everything but, really, we just know how to look things up. Talking to Regina is like talking to a hypochondria hotline.

What a brilliant idea. The library needed a hypochondria hotline. What a grabby, splashy, NEW idea. This would seal the deal and confirm Nan as an innovative librarian, not a regular old this-is-how-we've-always-done-it librarian.

Nan trotted right into work and started talking it up.

"People won't call a hotline." Mona frowned, shaking her head. "They want in-person service. They want to be waited on hand and foot. They want you to pull the book off the shelf, put it in their hands, point to the paragraph."

"Yeah, then they want us to copy it for them. They think they can't master a simple copier, but that's not true," Dunkan said. "I keep telling them it's easy, but no one believes me. I show them and I show them, and they say, 'You do it.'"

Nan thought they were dead wrong about a hypochondria hotline. She pictured insomniacs worrying all night and leaving messages about their strange-looking bowel movements, their itchy inner ears, that black freckle that hadn't been there yesterday. On second thought, she'd better turn off the message function so they had to call when the library was open, or this all could get out of hand quickly.

Nan loved medical research but only when no gory color photographs of internal organs or deformities were involved. She especially loved finding hefty research studies with the one little fact buried in them that was really the only thing the sick person wanted to know—how many people survived this disease. Everyone wanted to live. Everyone wanted their loved ones to live.

She had quickly figured out she could spend her whole budget buying medical and self-help books—that was how popular they were. She could never buy enough; people were ravenous devourers of books about their back problems, the latest theory on preventing cancer, the new diet to lower cholesterol or reverse diabetes. They were suckers for books with numbers in the title, like *Ten Steps to Blissful Sleep, Rewire Your Metabolism in Thirty Days, The One Minute Workout to Add One Hundred Years to Your Life.*

Oh, people, you're going to die anyway, Nan wanted to say. She should know, she was a Stage IV hypochondriac. She thought about death and dying more than she would ever admit to anyone (Stage IV), but at least she didn't bother doctors with every little pang (Stage V).

She couldn't wait to get started making library history with her hotline. This could be her claim to the Librarian Hall of Fame. Was there one?

CHAPTER NINE

HER NEXT VISIT to Russo's had nothing to do with T at all. Nan simply deserved a sweet Italian treat. After all, she was a trend-setting librarian *and* a thug-fighting ninja.

I am digging my grave with my teeth.

Where in the world did that come from? Barbara Pym, of course—from a sticky fruitcake encounter at a tea party in *Crampton Hodnet.* Did other people hear phrases from novels in their heads like this? Sometimes even with a British accent? Her brain amazed her with its secret weirdness.

Even though the town had three other Italian delis, everyone agreed Russo's cookies were the best. Nan deserved the best cookies; that was all. And she'd bring some home to Immaculata and Joe. They'd been feeding her so much, and it was the least she could do.

Russo's had them all on display: glazed lemon knots, butter sandwich cookies with chocolate hazelnut between layers, espresso florentines, pignoli cookies, almond ball wedding cookies covered in rainbow sprinkles, and orange ricotta cookies. Nan salivated just staring at them.

Loyalties to the delis were fierce; they all had more than enough business to keep going. Those who liked Zello's meatballs better than Di Genova's meatballs went to Zello's. Those who liked Piccolo's bread better than Luigi and Frank's bread went to Piccolo's. People who were extra fussy went from store to store picking the items they liked best from each place. Russo's salami, Di Genova's olives, Zello's stuffed shells, Luigi and Frank's sausage, and Piccolo's cream puffs made a perfect shopping expedition for a great Sunday dinner.

For once, the deli was relatively quiet. Nan leaned over the counter to talk to T.

"What's your best cookie? I've never had any of these."

T walked to the kitchen and came back with a tray of unwrapped cookies. She dipped her pinkie into the chocolate hazelnut spread oozing out of a sandwich cookie and slid it between Nan's lips.

So cornball. Yet so very effective. Nan laughed and sucked the sweetness from T's finger.

This woman never misses a trick. But I'm just here to buy cookies.

"So where are all the queers around here?" Nan asked. She hadn't run into many. Well, there was that one woman who dressed like a pharmaceutical rep, all sassy-corporate with breasts peeking out of low-cut tops, wearing very high heels to show off her spin-class-hardened legs. Every time she came to the library, she flicked her brown eyes at Nan with an unmistakable click of recognition, that old gaydar still working for both of them. Nan enjoyed her visits for that little thrill.

"Most of them leave when they turn eighteen, and they don't come back," T said, eating the rest of the cookie. "Not because their families throw them out. More because they were extremely bored here. They leave to find fun. Except me. I said, the hell with that; I'm staying. I make my own fun. Nobody's going to force me out. Plus, I know where all the bodies are buried; you know what I mean?"

"Not really," Nan said.

"I mean I know all the stories. I know the guy who got

married to a woman to put on a good show but keeps his boyfriend in an apartment across town. I know this woman who has a big old family, five kids who all look like chips off that old block of cheese, but has a girlfriend living in the mother-in-law suite pretending she's a nanny or a housekeeper. The wife sleeps with her most nights. What kind of household help is that?"

"Expensive," Nan said.

"I know the cops who talk a good game but take their motorcycles up to Philly every weekend to the leather bar—that's male and female cops both, by the way. And I know the brothers and sisters who've transitioned to sisters and brothers. They don't come back here to live. Their families go visit them where they are. I'm dying to see one of them come back to a school reunion as their new self. That would be so cool."

"Aren't you lonely here?" Nan missed her lost city friends. (Get in touch when you're back in the city, they'd all said as if she'd gone to live on the other side of the world instead of New Jersey.)

"Never. I get around. I'm always in a good mood because you know why? I'm right where I want to be. I got my shop. I got my looks. I got my motorcycle. I got everything."

Which is why I can never get involved with you, no

matter how desperate I am, Nan reminded herself. *You have not a thought in your head deeper than putting provolone on sale; your adorable tomboy haircut; your tan chiseled forearms that I bet you display all year, no matter the temperature; and your cute butchy flirty self. Oh, I am straying into bad territory here.*

"Hey, Philly, you're lonely, then?" T asked. "I can help you fix that."

Oh, for god's sake, did she just wink at me?

"Do you ever stop flirting? Do you ever have a normal conversation?" Nan asked.

"Not if I can help it. You know you love it."

I do kind of love it. But I am working on a new life here, and you are so not a part of it.

Nan forced herself back to work.

*

"THAT GUY LIVES in a tent in the woods," the assistants whispered to Nan.

Only one homeless person in a public library? That was some kind of record. Nan resolved to treat him like every other library user, not avoid eye contact or small talk just because he lived in a tent.

"Hi, did you find what you were looking for today?" She wandered over to stand by the seat in the far corner he'd claimed for himself, glaring at anyone who sat there until they moved. God forbid if anyone needed a book on puppetry. They'd have to climb over him to get to it.

The man looked up, startled. He smelled like smoke and dirty male body, but his odor wasn't horrific; it was bearable.

Bearable—what a funny word, Nan pondered. Was it supposed to have anything to do with bears?

"The orbs are circling," he finally hissed. "They'll pick someone up tonight."

Nan sat down beside him. "Who are they?" She genuinely wanted to know. She watched his face twitch with the urge to share his news as he fought with his distaste for talking to other humans.

"Planetary visitors," he finally said.

"Have you seen them?" She'd always wanted to talk to someone who'd seen a UFO up close. She had a sneaking suspicion they were real.

He shook no, then nodded an urgent yes. He kept that up, his head bobbing hard up and down and then sideways, until she got up and left, afraid it would topple off at that rate.

She couldn't stop thinking about UFOs all day. For a few

months last year, she'd read every book on the subject she could get her hands on. It was one of the reading jags she indulged in regularly: biographies of Victorian women adventurers, true crime (but only when men were the murder victims; she was sick of reading about slaughtered women), reincarnation, anything even mentioning Eleanor Roosevelt, to name a few.

That night, she left all her lights on as a protective shield and sat out on the landing by her front door, a triple-layer afghan wrapped around her. She had a long unobstructed view from there, fields and woods in three directions and town buildings in the other. Surely, the visitors would come to the fields or woods. Surely, they wouldn't circle over a town. They were smarter than that. So many witness accounts described alien visitors hovering over remote roads beside woods to minimize attention. All of the UFO accounts took place late at night.

"What are you doing up there? Turn off them lights. Go to bed," Immaculata's voice shouted from below.

"I'm your tenant, not your child," Nan yelled back. "Are you losing your marbles? You can't tell me what to do."

"We don't have kids. Joe shoots blanks, thank god."

Did I ask you to share Joe's sperm count?

"In case you forgot, you got work in the morning," Immaculata said.

"In case you forgot, I don't answer to you."

Immaculata laughed. Nan knew she loved nothing more than a sparring match.

"I'm waiting for aliens to land," Nan said. "I have good information sources that say it will be tonight."

Immaculata came shooting out the back door. She grabbed the stair railing and hoisted her body up the steps.

"I'm coming up; I'm bored of making pizzelles," she said.

Nan had heard the whole pizzelle story from Immaculata: how she made bags and bags of those anisette-flavored pressed cookies every week for the local bakery and only charged them for the cost of her materials, how Joe delivered them every Friday and was always after her to raise her prices that were still the same after ten years. But Immaculata refused, afraid the stores would stop the orders, and then she'd have too much time on her hands.

"Who invited you to my alien party?" Nan asked.

"It's my house; it's my steps."

"You need a basic course in being a landlord. Do you want me to bring you a library book on that? Chapter One, don't bother your tenants."

"Ha ha, funny librarian," Immaculata said. "So what's the story?"

"There's a guy who lives in the Pine Barrens in a tent. He comes in a few times a week to read the *Wall Street Journal* and *Business Week*. He says the orbs are circling, and to-night's the night they'll pick someone up."

"I'll go up in the sky with aliens," Immaculata said. "What do I have to lose?"

"Are you kidding me? You haven't left your house in how long? Fifty years?" Nan was astonished to hear Immaculata even joke about leaving.

"Because there's nothing I haven't seen in town. What do I need to go there for? But there's a lot I haven't seen up there." She pointed overhead. "I heard a story about up there—from my great-grandfather."

"I need more wine for this." Nan filled her own glass and held out the jug to Immaculata, who shook her head.

"I can't drink too much, it gives me agita," she said.

"Upsets your stomach?"

"No, I get aggravated in my head; I get belligerent. Joe said to knock it off, so I did."

"More for me," Nan said.

Immaculata flapped her hand dismissively at Nan and

continued. "My great-grandfather was off-the-boat Italian, came here to work in the fields back when Italians were like the Mexicans are today. They worked them like dogs, but they were tough. The Italians had a million kids, their kids had lots more kids, and now we run the damn town. Anyway, when he was ninety-nine years old, he leaned over to me and whispered a story in my ear. He said, 'I come from another planet, not Italy. I come from a beautiful place up in the sky. There, the nights are green, not black. There, the water runs in black-and-white stripes, not blue. There, the air itself is food. You don't have to eat or drink; the air gives you everything you need. It's wonderful there. Soon, I'll be going back to my planet.'"

"Wow, what did you think of that?" Nan was astonished at the picture the man had painted.

"He only had a fourth-grade education. I couldn't believe he even knew what a planet was, let alone had the brains left to make up a story like that. So it must be true," Immaculata said, shrugging.

"Could be. We don't know everything."

"You think you know everything, your head full of books," Immaculata said.

"What's your head full of, old lady?" Nan really wanted

to know. How could someone live a life in one house and yard, rarely leaving? How could someone be happy who wasn't a reader? What the heck did Immaculata even think about?

"My head is full of nonsense, just like everybody else." Immaculata got up slowly and clumped downstairs, turning her head to shout, "Go to bed. Them aliens aren't coming tonight."

Maybe aliens would show up, who knew? Everything was unexpected here. Nan thought of the town with a lower-case *t*, one of the many weirdo small towns in South Jersey, tucked among the Pine Barrens National Reserve, where bodies of murder victims from Philadelphia, Newark, and Atlantic City were often found months later in shallow graves under the scrub pines or surfacing in one of the lakes. Sure, there were beautiful blueberry and cranberry bogs, historic village museums, walking trails, and other scenic things, but Nan liked to think of the area mainly as a murder dumping ground. She read a lot of mysteries, so when she walked, she was always on the lookout for a floating body in the bog.

She had discovered that people who lived here pronounced it Town with a capital *T*, saying its name, Pinetree, with evident reverence. If she had a nickel for every time she'd been asked "Are you from Town?" she'd be a rich woman. She wanted to ask them: "What town? This isn't the only town on earth. Maybe I'm from another town, did you ever think of that?"

What kind of town was this town, anyway? She was learning this was a town where kids gave one another nicknames in childhood that held up for a whole lifetime. This was a town of hunters, where when driving down a back road during the right time of year, it was normal to see a lodge porch with three dead deer hanging upside down from hooks, the road flanked by an army of men holding shotguns walking into the brush in formation. This was a town where a guy they called "The Arsonist," as if it was his job title, would burn a business down or set a car on fire if the owner shared the insurance money with him. This was a town of farmers, where ninety-year-olds were still running tractors, proud to be known for their fat worm-free broccoli and juicy tomatoes.

For Nan, this town was as foreign as another planet. She was the alien plopped down here. Would she ever get used to it?

CHAPTER TEN

WHEN THE RED-HAIRED boy with a face full of freckles walked into the library, Nan noticed him right away. He was alone, which made him noticeable at the age when most kids moved in packs like schools of fish, roaming from school to library to dollar store to deli in a wavy group formation. He was a redhead in a town full of dark-haired Italian Americans. He was bone-thin, in a town of well-fed children. He was dressed in worn clothes and old shoes, a thrift-shop look about him.

When she asked if she could help him find anything, he hung his head and shook no, a perfect imitation of a puppy dog who'd chewed up something he shouldn't have.

"I'm right here if you decide you need a hand with any-thing," Nan said, despising her own fake-sounding heartiness.

"Why?" he asked, his voice small and wavering.

"It's my job. I help everyone in here," she said, wishing she came across as sincere as she really was. She hated her voice. It sounded exactly like her sisters' voices, as much as she tried to make it different. It must be the way their wide flat noses were constructed.

"Why are you being so nice to me?" he whispered.

She was so startled she dropped the pen she was holding. He picked it up for her.

"I mean the other librarian at school is a stone hard-ass bitch."

"She's not a librarian," Nan corrected him. "She's just a volunteer."

She'd met the woman, introduced to her as the middle school librarian, Concetta Spitilli. But when Nan asked the question that all librarian conversations started with ("So where'd you go to library school?"), the woman had sniffed as if there was a bad smell in the air and said she hadn't gone to graduate school at all. She'd been recruited to take over as a volunteer many years ago when the school decided to save money by eliminating the school librarian position. Because after all, the public library was right across the street, and *they* had to have a librarian with a master's degree to get state aid funding, but the school didn't. So that was enough librarians for this town.

"I did it to help out when my daughter was here, and I stayed on when she graduated. And I certainly don't need a graduate degree to run this place," Concetta had said dismissively. "I have a cadre of volunteers to help me."

I'll give you a half point for vocabulary. I don't know the last time I've heard the word "cadre" spoken in casual conversation. But that's all the credit I'll give you, well-meaning as you may be.

Nan could rant all day long about the use of unqualified volunteers in libraries. How people assumed anyone could be a librarian. How good-hearted women (it was always women) with time on their hands loved to fuss with books and read children stories. How the result was that all the important things a well-run library could do were weakened as volunteers not acquainted with the basic foundations of librarianship (freedom to read whatever you want, access to information for all, privacy and confidentiality, diversity, and other tenets) simply made it all up as they went along, with the results being crappy excuses for real libraries. As a library manager, Nan had vowed she would never use volunteers because it sent the wrong message to government officials who controlled library budgets.

To the boy, Nan added, "Don't say bitch, please."

I just said the word I told him not to say. Way to go, genius.

"Sorry—she's a witch," he corrected himself.

"Why are you whispering?" Nan whispered. "You can talk in a low tone in here." Even though she wasn't. She was still whispering to make him comfortable.

"That witch, Ms. Spitface, said I couldn't read a book I picked out. She took it out of my hands, said it was too hard for me."

Nan was outraged on his behalf. "I can't believe even a volunteer would do that."

"Well, she did. She doesn't even know my reading level. I just started at this school. I am off the charts in reading, but that witch never bothered to ask. My last school tested me. They said I was reading on a college level, and I'm only in seventh grade."

The way he pronounced "college level" made it clear to her it was as big a deal to him as "free unlimited ice cream" would be to another kid his age.

"Okay, I get it," Nan said. "How about we make a deal. You don't call people bad names in here, and I'll let you take out any book you want. I swear."

"What about them?" he asked, pointing to the front desk assistants.

"They work for me. We have policies set by the national library association that say we believe people can read whatever they want, even kids. If your parents want to forbid you taking out a book, they can come with you and dictate what you can read. But we can't and won't. We are not your parents. We are defenders of your right to read. We eat censorship for breakfast."

He smiled a big freckly smile, disappeared into the 300 section, and came back seconds later with a sex manual, *How to Satisfy Any Woman*. It had been a big bestseller a few years back. Now it sat sadly on the shelf. Apparently, everyone who'd wanted to read it had already found it, practiced, and returned it for others to enjoy. Nan wondered if she'd learn anything new if she read it.

"What if I take this out? Are you going to let me?" he dared her.

"Are your parents with you?"

"I don't live with them."

"Who's in charge of you?"

"I'm in a group home for foster kids. Nobody's in charge of me."

Great, no angry parents will show up to yell at me this time.

Nan took the book out of his hand and walked it over to the desk. He pulled his library card out of his pocket and handed it to her with a flourish. She checked it out herself, so that Mona or Dunkan didn't have a chance to question it. His name was Jeremy Murphy, she noted.

"Happy reading, Jeremy," she said, handing him the book. "See you later. Thanks for coming in."

He stared at her as if waiting for her to snatch the book back from him, backed out to the front door keeping his eyes on her, then turned and ran out like someone was chasing him.

"What was that all about?" Mona asked.

"You know we don't act in loco parentis," Nan said.

"But that was not a book for kids."

"So what? We don't forbid kids to take out other books above their grade level. That little guy who reads the chess books. That girl who's building her own boat—she takes out those how-to books from the adult library. We don't even call it the adult library. It's all the library." Nan used her firmest voice and body language to make it clear this point was not negotiable.

A woman with her hair wrapped in pink foam curlers straight out of the 1950s plopped her books from the new book section down on the desk. "He could probably write a book on the subject anyhow. All these kids today know more than I ever did before I got married," she cackled. "I could tell you stories."

Please don't.

Nan stared at the middle school across the street, wondering what other harms the library volunteer had inflicted on eager readers. She vowed to take Jeremy under her wing and save him as the kind librarians had saved her when she was a kid with a mother who cried a lot.

But how?

CHAPTER ELEVEN

NAN WAS DYING to set up the Hypochondria Hotline. She pictured splashy posters and flyers, lots of talking it up at the front desk, maybe a billboard out on the highway. But she couldn't because of the stinking schedule.

After the urination incident, she needed to staff the Children's Room every single second they were open. No more of this popping in every so often from upstairs. She didn't care how quiet it was down there; a staff person had to be stationed there. She was never going to clean up pee-ruined books again.

Scheduling was a nightmare. She had to approve so many

changes every week that she felt her brain melting from the stress of it. These people filled out the change/leave requests practically daily, it seemed. All Nan cared about was that there were enough people in the building so no one was alone during break and lunch times. Because that seemed critical to her. Small town or no small town, it was not safe to leave a woman alone in a public building for an hour. The full-time staff was all women except for Dunkan.

Some days, it seemed all Nan did was tinker with the schedule. It was exhausting and mind-numbing. She thought briefly about delegating the schedule to her chief assistant. But Mona didn't even pretend she would be neutral and fair. She was a woman for whom a whiff of power was as intoxicating as an entire bottle of champagne.

When something didn't work right, it was the process that was at fault, Nan knew. She thought about the scheduling process endlessly. There must be a way to make this work more smoothly.

First, she circulated a blank online calendar to the staff and asked each assistant to enter their dream schedule on it, one they'd stick to every week. Dunkan wanted to work all nights and weekends. He was like a vampire; he wanted to come out when others went home. Mona wanted to work only weekdays. So the two of them were a perfect match of opposites, on the surface of it. If only the others would be so easy.

She had staff who were caring for children, grandchildren, parents, grandparents. There were three single mothers, including Trixie Termino, who was famous for giving birth in the library after being in complete denial that she could be pregnant at forty-nine. Now, Trixie was dating the EMT who'd caught the baby boy as he emerged right in front of the new book section. Nan wasn't surprised to hear that story. Trixie was not what she would call an alert woman living in the present. Her face often wore the blank smile of a mannequin, and her mind seemed to be floating above it all.

Many of the staff had other jobs because the pay at the library was mostly minimum wage or a little above for those who had been there for a long time. Even Mona worked shifts at her husband's combination jewelry store and bowling alley when he needed her. Nan had a real mess on her hands to make it all work.

The library had to stay flexible with all these people as it was so hard to find others to replace them. The current employees were trained, experienced, friendly, helpful—most of the time anyway. They only stayed on at the library because it had always bent to their schedules. They didn't get paid much, but they did get all the holidays and a schedule they could massage.

Nan had to solve this. The library was getting busier and busier, especially since she'd ordered a huge sign to hang outside by the front door. No one could miss it. In giant block letters, the sign read "FREE Books, Movies, Music Inside. Don't Give Your Money to Internet Zillionaires. They Have Enough." In smaller letters, "Library=Your Tax Dollars at Work." The minute it went up, she saw two cars full of people pull over, everyone pointing at the sign. Nan felt triumphant. Enlightenment, one person at a time.

Finally, she asked the staff, "What if I put up a blank schedule every month and you fill in when you want to work? It doesn't have to be the same every week. As long as there are three people on the schedule for every minute we're open and you don't exceed your weekly hours, you can work when you want."

"I vote yes," Mona said, her eyes gleaming.

"It's not as easy as it sounds," Nan said. "I've been struggling to make this work for everyone."

"We can do it," Dunkan said. "I like being in charge of my own schedule."

"Piece of cake," Trixie said. "Oh, that makes me hungry.

THE NEW TOWN LIBRARIAN - 103 -

Does anyone have a piece of cake?" That stopped the conversation—her specialty.

The new schedule failed miserably and immediately. Nan saw big gaps the very first month, where no one had signed up to fill the slots.

"What's wrong?" she asked. "I thought you all wanted to try this."

"I filled in what I wanted," Dunkan said. "But Mona erased it."

"Because you can't work all nights and weekends," Mona said. "You have to leave some for other people."

"Nobody wants that but me," he protested.

"You have to give them a chance," Mona insisted. "You can't hog all the nights and weekends."

"I'm not putting in for days if I don't want days. I hate getting up early."

"That's not fair," Mona said.

"You don't want to work nights and weekends anyway. Why can't I?"

Nan watched, fascinated. Dunkan was actually standing up for himself.

"I might want to sometime. Maybe on my husband's poker night. Maybe when he's having a football party on a weekend," Mona said. "I've been here twenty years. You've been here twenty minutes. Why should you get all the say?"

Dunkan looked on the edge of tears. That would never do. Nan wanted him to keep feeling his power. She called the meeting to a halt.

"I'll work more on this," she said. "For now, when I post a schedule, please follow it. When you need to request a change, put it on the form as usual."

Nan's dream of running a library all by herself did not center on making and remaking schedules all day, holding endless staff meetings about details like this. She had dreamed of creating a perfect book collection, achieving record-setting circulation statistics, winning awards for best town library in the state, earning grants for cultural programming that would bring standing-room-only crowds.

She walked over to the hardware store, hoping to find Chuck Hornfeck in. He was always happy to see her and loved to talk over what was going on at the library.

"Just between us," she started after they were seated in his office, with coffee in hand. "I have one word for you. Scheduling." She could tell by the look on his face that he'd been there.

"Tell me about it," he said. "I spend half my life working

on the store schedule."

"We went to graduate school for this," she said.

"I know. No one tells you management is 50 percent scheduling."

"I wish mine were 50 percent. Some days, it feels like 85," she said. "People."

"What can you do," he agreed.

They shook their heads and went on to talk of other things. As always, she left feeling better. He was a lovely man. She could talk to him all day. He was always reading something interesting, and he had a way of talking about what he was reading in an enticing way, not droning on, not boasting of his intellect. She wondered about his wife, what their conversations were like. She'd never met his wife but had heard she didn't read.

How sad was that. This man's face lit up when he talked about books. How could he be married to someone who didn't read?

On second thought, Nan had been in a relationship with a woman who ran her family's pickle company and read only books on new things to pickle. (Pickled blueberries? Pickled pumpkin? Yuck.) Which didn't even count as books as far as she was concerned. They were overblown feature articles with large graphics thrown in to make more pages, to make the tiny bit of relevant content seem worth paying for a hardback book. What a colossal waste of paper.

But who was she to judge what others read or didn't read? She really didn't care that much. She loved books and had her own all-involving relationship with them. Sometimes it was a tumultuous relationship, with her ending up deeply disappointed in a book by a favorite author, a book that showed all too clearly that when you achieved a big literary reputation and were a best-selling author, no one dared to edit you too closely. There were a few authors who had flown so high no one could cut them down, and it showed.

Late that night, Chuck's face popped into her head again, along with a fantastic idea—she would form a secret book club and ask Chuck to be in it. Secret because she didn't want others trying to invite themselves. Secret because she didn't want it to be an official library book club. She wanted only to have people there she actually wanted to talk to.

"I love how you talk about books," she said in an email to Chuck. "How about a book club where we read whatever we want to and then we get together to talk about them? A different kind of book club where we don't have to agree to read the same book at the same time, just enthusiasts who enjoy talking about what they read. What do you think?"

He wrote back immediately, "Yes!!!"

For the next few days, she made a point to come out of her office regularly when she heard the voices of readers she'd talked to before. Each one, she considered for her secret book club.

She almost asked Lolly Fizzarella, the ebullient president of the Friends of the Library group, an inveterate athlete who Nan had only ever seen wearing running tights. Lolly was in the library all the time, often ran there wearing a backpack and ran home with it loaded up with books for herself and her six kids, looking like a woman in basic training. She ran to every meeting the Friends had, and she ran back home at the end of their meetings too. But Lolly intimidated her. The two of them were so different. Nan worried incessantly; Lolly was so full of endorphins she wouldn't know a worry if it bopped her in the face.

Nan wished she didn't like Lolly so much. She'd like to disparage her Rebecca of Sunnybrook Farm demeanor and her enthusiastic outlook on life, but she couldn't. She was a perfect woman. Nan wished she were Lolly. Maybe she should run like Lolly; maybe she'd run into happiness that way.

Her secret book club would not help her with her schedule problems, with blocking the mad urinator from a return visit to the Children's Room, with the terror of a creating a budget, or with setting up the Hypochondria Hotline. But like cookies, Nan needed to dangle a treat for her soul, a reward up ahead for the hard stuff. She was almost at her ninety-day review point. If she got past that, she was officially a permanent employee. She willed herself to stay on task, and then she'd reward herself with all manner of wild times.

*

NAN FELT LIKE a hurdler gearing up to leap over the biggest obstacle of her life, the dreaded library budget. First, she had to present it to the library board of trustees, then to the town council. Math had been her worst subject her whole life. Numbers flew right out of her brain the minute they entered.

But this task had already been done before her many times. She figured she would copy the budget from the previous year, repeating each line item, and then start adjusting it to reflect her goals for the next year. The librarian before her had been organized, so the files, both digital and paper, were all in order.

It went well for the first few categories as they were clear and understandable. Staff positions, wages, and salaries un-spooled before her, giving her a lovely bounce of confidence. She built in two new library assistant positions, one full-time and one part-time, so that when the powers-that-be cut one out (as they were sure to do, it was as tempting as killing birds is to a cat), she'd still have an extra body to throw at the per-ennially problematic monthly schedule.

Books and materials were easy. She revised both amounts upward to make their new materials budget exceed what the state guidelines called for. This was fun; this was why she became a librarian in the first place.

The troubles began when she got to all the boring budget lines: telecommunications, supplies, equipment repair, utili-ties. How was she supposed to estimate and plan for those? She didn't even know what they each meant, really. How could she know what equipment would break in the upcom-ing year? Was she supposed to be psychic? What kind of con-trol did anyone have over utilities and telecommunication in-creases? They went up annually willy-nilly, it seemed to her. Was she just supposed to make numbers up?

She was getting incredibly tired and hungry. She had de-cided she'd have to work on the budget after the library was closed at 8:00 p.m. because of the constant interruptions when they were open. The silence and darkness of the empty building was bliss, but it was also nod-producing; she had turned off most of the lights except for the ones in her office.

She needed caffeine and went to the staff room to raid the refrigerator. If she drank someone else's diet soda, she'd replace it first thing tomorrow. If she was so lucky as to find a leftover hoagie, she'd give whoever left it a raise.

On her way to the staff room, she found a poetry book propped up on the floor in front of the bathroom with the title *From the Land of Despair.*

What am I going to do about these dire messages? Someone is definitely leaving them for me to find.

She heard a tapping on the front door with something metallic and peeked around the corner to see T waving at her, keys in hand. Nan unlocked the door, and T came in with a grocery bag.

"Are you a vegetarian?" T asked. "I feel like you put out that vegetarian vibe, but I wasn't sure."

"No, I eat meat. But not too much. Same with fish, only once in a while. It's not like I have anything against meat or fish; I just don't crave them much. But I feel like I don't want to be a vegetarian all the way. It seems too picky. And a good old Philly cheesesteak—even saying the words makes my mouth water."

Why am I yammering on and on? It's a simple question.

"Cool. I brought a bunch of stuff for you."

T handed her the grocery bag. It smelled divine. Nan wanted to rip it open and dig in, she was so ravenous.

"Why?" Nan asked. "It's not my birthday. Do you always run around town bringing food to random strangers?"

"Like you're a stranger. You're famous. Town Librarian, that's a big job around here."

"Really, what's up?"

"I was leaving work. I saw your light. Thought you might like to have dinner with me."

"Here, in the library?"

"Why not? You're working late; I was doing inventory; I'm starving. How about you?"

Nan admitted that she was.

"I got wine in here too," T said. "Emergency wine. Just in case."

"Of what?"

"In case we need it."

Hearing the word "we," Nan's legs went wobbly. *Dammit, this is not what I need right now. I'm on probation. And this woman is unsuitable. Absolutely no future here. This will end as badly as all my other ridiculous affairs and relation-ships.*

But then again, my favorite wise woman, Barbara Pym, recognized how absurd and delicious it is to be in love with someone younger than yourself and advised everybody to try it. Why not me, why not now?

Nan remembered being in bed with her last ex, Pebbles. The way sex with Pebbles had always felt like trying to get a gas lawnmower going, the need to pull harder again and again, the sputtering choking starts as the gas started to trickle where it needed to go, the disappointment as it failed to catch, then restarting again and again until her anger came roaring up. *Why isn't this working? It worked great with every other woman I've ever been with. What's wrong with you? What's wrong with us?* In the end, Nan decided Pebbles was a cold person. It didn't matter why—whether it was her body chemistry, her upbringing, or her psychological patterns. Cold was cold. She had walked away finally, but she believed that failed relationship had poisoned her sexual life for years since then. Five long years, in fact.

Nan and T went downstairs and sat on beanbags in the Children's Room without discussing it. It was the only place where no one was likely to see them as the windows were so high up.

I'm starving; she brought food. That's all this is, a lovely dinner.

They leaned their backs against the low picture-book shelves. Nan placed a flashlight on the floor so they wouldn't have to turn on the overhead lights. She didn't want to draw attention to their presence in case the police decided to make a security check on the library, for once in their lives.

A picnic in a dark library, this was the most fun Nan had had in a very long time. She always knew she had fun in her, but it had gone so deep inside she'd lost touch with it. It was delicious to feel fun pop up again.

After the bottle of deep-red wine was gone, after the picnic of soft cheese (how had she gotten to the age of fifty without ever tasting Taleggio?), pane di Lariano bread, cacciatore salami, marinated mozzarella balls, hot olive salad, and grilled Roman artichokes, Nan pulled T close to her and kissed her full on the mouth. This feast, this woman, there was nothing else for her to do.

It had been a long five years in a sexual desert. Nan had been wandering thirsty and needy, hoping for an oasis of a woman like this but unable to make it happen. Now she cared about nothing but quenching her mighty thirst.

Two hours later, T said, "You're welcome, Philly." She smiled a huge smile, pulling her clothes back on.

Did I say thank you out loud? Nan rolled to a wobbly standing position. *Oh, that's a little embarrassing.*

It didn't matter. Nothing mattered except the blessed relief of this moment. Everything still worked, every part of her sang. She was a magnificent beast of a woman, no one had caught them in the act, and best of all, she had incredible leftovers to bring home for a midnight feast.

*

THE VERY NEXT day, right before her ninety-day probation was up, Nan was summoned to Pip Conti's office for a meeting. She had pestered his administrative assistant about the subject of the meeting, refusing to hang up until the woman sighed and said it was something to do with the middle school library.

Whew, not our sex picnic in the Children's Room. A tsunami of relief washed over Nan. If she was let go at the end of her probation, she'd rather it be for any other reason. Something a tad less unseemly than being overcome by lust in a public building.

She bounce-walked from happiness to Pip's office. Now

that was a job title, Superintendent of Schools. It sounded like he managed a vast network, but there were only three teeny-weeny schools in Pinetree: an elementary, a middle, and a high school.

"We have a situation," he began.

We? Maybe you do. I'm feeling swell.

"Concetta Spitilli, our middle school librarian..." he said.

Nan wanted to interrupt him by correcting to, *She's just a volunteer,* but she forced herself to keep her mouth shut.

"She is no longer...able to run the library. So we'd like you to take that on."

An arrow of pain shot into Nan's forehead.

"You're right across the street, after all. You can run over there and teach library skills and staff the library during school hours. I'm sure you'll do a fine job," he said encouragingly.

Nan pictured herself as a giant librarian astride Central Avenue, one foot planted in one building and one in the other, one long arm in each library. This was an untenable and outrageous proposition. He wanted two librarians for the price of one. School librarians had totally different certifications, skills, and education than public librarians. She didn't even like children. She hated teaching anything. She hated how schools always smelled so sweaty. She was utterly screwed. How would she get herself out of this?

Her throat throbbed with the urge to scream how unfair this was. This was why she'd always preferred to be the lowest librarian on the ladder. No one noticed her, no one made her do things she didn't want to do, and no one made her fight battles with powerful people at the top.

"This should be easy for you. A few lessons a day, a different budget to manage. That's all," he said.

Easy. You know what would be easy? To pick up that big paperweight on your desk and smash your head in. Happens all the time in village murder mysteries.

She struggled to keep her voice neutral. "To clarify, you would like me to run two separate libraries at the same time?" For the same ridiculous low pay.

He nodded as though he were pleased with how quickly she'd caught on to his scheme.

"When are you planning to replace Concetta? If this is a very short-term arrangement..." Nan's heart pounded as if she were being held at gunpoint.

"No plans," he answered breezily. "We'll see."

We'll see how far we can push you, that's what he means. Well, two can play this game. You pompous nitwit. You scourge of my work life. You ignoramus.

"We'll see," Nan repeated as pleasantly as she could. *That means nothing. My mother used to say that when she didn't want to answer our questions. (Can we go to the library now? Can we have ice cream for lunch?) I'm using it to establish a holding pattern, awaiting landing in my new life.*

He thought she was powerless. He was going to find out what happened when you push an older woman too far, a woman with everything to lose.

CHAPTER TWELVE

SHE HAD A secret weapon for getting information on the middle school library situation—Jeremy. Nan had been making a point to sit down with him every day, ask him what he was reading, what his homework was about, and to listen when he answered. He seemed starved for attention and mortified by it at the same time. His freckled face got red when she came over and stayed red the whole time she talked with him.

"I have to do a book report. They're all reading baby books, but I picked this one. Not from the school library, from here." He showed her a hardback copy of Daniel Defoe's *Robinson Crusoe*. The cover showed a burly man in ragged clothes, standing on a shore, looking woefully up at seagulls.

"I remember that one," Nan said.

He looked shocked. "You read that? It's a boy book, isn't it?"

"There's no such thing."

She wondered if Concetta Spitilli had organized the school library into boy books and girl books during her tenure. Nan wouldn't have been surprised at that level of ineptitude. Ignorance, pure and simple.

"Why would a girl read this book?" Jeremy asked.

"I love runaways. I used to read every book I could find about runaways when I was your age. And orphans. I was dying to be an orphan."

"Ha ha," he said. "Dying to be an orphan."

He had a sense of humor, Nan realized.

"I had two older sisters I couldn't stand," she said. "So I wished they would disappear, and my parents too, then I could go off on my own and make my way in the world as an orphan."

When he looked down, his smile faded. She was furious at herself for her tactlessness. He was an actual orphan or might as well be. She changed the subject.

"So how do you like *Robinson Crusoe* so far?"

"I already finished it," he said with a proud little smile. "It's my favorite book so far in life, and I've read a lot of books. I'm going to read it a few more times just for fun. When I write this report, I'll get an A-plus for sure."

Nan wanted to say, oh little man, don't expect that; don't expect anything. *For the cause of all unhappiness in life is expectation*, as Buddhism taught. She wondered what Jeremy's story was. How did he end up in foster care? Would he ever be reunited with his family? That was the bad thing about working with the public; she heard only parts of their story and never knew how the people she met ended up.

"Hey, Jeremy, help me out." She lowered her voice and leaned closer. His clothes smelled unpleasant, as if they'd been slept in for many days. He gave off a nasty whiff of unwashed boy.

"What happened to Ms. Spitilli anyway?" She bet he would know. He had probably been there when it happened. This kid was attracted to anywhere books were.

He shrugged. "She said she wasn't into it anymore. She said she wasn't going to put up with our crap for no money, so she left. She said she wasn't coming back ever again. And she called us little dirtbags."

"So who's in charge of the school library, then?"

"Nobody. The other ladies wouldn't do it without her. The teachers said no way, and they're in a union, so nobody can make them. The principal locked it."

So, Pip Conti is pretty desperate right about now. I'm going to use that.

Mona was waiting for her in her office with her I-am-going-tell-you-something-important face on. "It's Saturday, 4:45 p.m., and it's almost time to close."

"And?"

Make your point, Mona.

"Jeremy has been here since we opened at 9:00 a.m. He didn't leave for lunch. He hasn't eaten all day."

"Maybe he's not hungry." Nan wasn't accustomed to the mysterious ways of children.

"A boy his age needs to be fed regularly. Believe me. I raised six of them. They ate constantly. They need an incredible amount of food in them to grow. Just look at him; he's so thin. It breaks my heart."

Mona had a heart? This was news.

"What do you want me to do about it?" Nan was genuinely baffled.

"Handle it. He's in here every Saturday all day long. Plus on schooldays, he stays after school for hours all the way through dinnertime, through evening hours, then he leaves all by himself in the dark. We are not babysitters for hungry children. We are not dumping grounds for neglected children. It's outrageous. Something is very wrong with his living situation. You need to notify someone. Do something immediately before something terrible happens."

The last line in Nan's job description floated up from her subconscious: Other duties as assigned.

"I'll take care of it." She stood up to end the conversation.

But how would she take care of it? Her heart thumped painfully in her chest. Was it possible to literally die of worry? She was absolutely battered down by this latest worry, piled on top of all the others. The worst thing was she knew Mona was right. She'd noticed all of the same things about Jeremy but had chosen to push the thoughts away.

On her way home, Nan passed a dead deer twisted up in an impossible position and then a dead cat whose fur fluttered in the breeze in a shockingly macabre way. A record day for roadkill. She felt as bad as the perished animals looked.

A pain as hard as a brick slammed into the back of her

head. This was all too much. She wanted to be taken care of. She wanted tenderness to flow toward her. She wanted someone else to make everything all right.

When she got home, she caught Immaculata inside her apartment, in her bedroom, looking in her closet.

It didn't even seem all that strange a sight. This kind of thing happened when walls fell down, when lines were crossed so often you forgot they were ever there.

Instead of raging at Immaculata, Nan shocked herself by opening her arms silently, asking for a hug, then bursting into tears when Immaculata gave her a long brusque one. It was like hugging a wide-trunked tree. But she smelled so good (butter cookies and coffee) and felt so solid Nan hated to let go of her.

"Well, you don't have to cry about it. It was no big deal," Immaculata said. "I like to clean. I wanted to make the apartment nice for you."

And snoop while you were at it.

Nan didn't have the strength to do anything but collapse at the kitchen table and let Immaculata bring her a plate full of the most beautiful food she'd ever seen.

"I brought up manicotti and stuffed mushrooms since I was coming up anyway," she said.

I'm so needy. I'm so tired. I'm so grateful. What invasion of privacy? What landlord-tenant rules of conduct? I give up, Immaculata. I need help, and you're it.

Immaculata didn't disappoint. "That Pip Conti has let power go to his head. He goes around telling the mayor what to do, town council, everyone. He thinks he's in charge of the world."

"Not just me?" Nan joked. Telling Immaculata every single thing that was on her mind had been a huge relief.

"Stand up to him," Immaculata said. "If the rest of them fools would, he wouldn't be such a jerk. They just let him have his way because they're too lazy to fight with him all the time."

"What about Jeremy? I hate to report him to social services before I know what's going on. What if the group home manager makes him stay away from the library? The library is the only good thing in that kid's life. It's saving him." Nan knew in her bones that was true. She had been that kid too. Hanging out in the library all the time had saved her from her home with a sad mother and awful sisters.

"One step at a time," Immaculata said. "The only thing you need to do right now is feed him. I'll send you with extra."

Nan had not admitted to herself that Immaculata had begun handing her a lunch bag every day when she left for work like she was a kid in grade school again. It sounded so crazy, a landlady packing lunch for her tenant. But it was so good. It was right there, ready for her every day. It was irresistible to Nan—exotic Italian lunchmeats on the tastiest sesame seed rolls, fancy cut raw veggies with a swoon-worthy garlic aioli to dip them in, and homemade oatmeal-and-chocolate-chip cookies. She'd be happy to slip a bag of delights to Jeremy every day and find him a private place to eat it.

As for Pip, her chance to stand up to him came the very next day, the first day she was an official, permanent town employee. She felt untouchable now, a woman on top of the world.

No one else had made a big deal about her appointment. She was summoned to sign paperwork in Town Hall; that was all. But the step meant everything to her. She had many plans, starting with resistance against Pip Conti by any means necessary.

The phone rang as she was writing up a press release for the classic books lunchtime lecture series she'd been awarded funding for, having beat out way bigger and richer libraries.

Take that, Princeton Public Library. You may have a gorgeous mural by artist Ik-Joong Kang, "Happy World," lining your entrance and be the most visited municipal public library in the entire state, but we won this time.

"I'm calling from the middle school office. You need to come get the eighth-graders," a harried voice in her ear said. "You're late. They're ripping up the library. We unlocked it for you. Mr. Conti said you were on the schedule today."

"Nope. He misspoke. I don't work there," Nan said, hanging up. That felt better than the buzz from a goblet of Joe's best wine.

Five minutes later, a riot broke out by the front door. Thirty kids were pushing inside, then shoving one another, throwing hats, fighting over chairs and computers, calling one another names, and running through the narrow aisles. No one was touching a book. There appeared to be no adult with them, no teacher, no school staff, no security guard.

Nan watched for a minute, then called the police. "We have a riot situation at the library," she said. "You better hurry up."

She called Mona and Dunkan into her office and told them to wait there. She wasn't going to try to control the kids, and she wouldn't let them either. There were a few adults who had been using the computers, but they quickly left when they were jostled by the gang of kids. The same with the preschool-ers and their caregivers who had been in the Children's

Room. One of the moms came up to see what all the noise was and saw that no one was in charge of the kids. Then the sound of the emergency alarm went off as the mom left by the downstairs security door. Nan didn't blame them a bit.

When the library liaison officer opened the front door, she quickly closed it again and called for backup. A few minutes later, Nan heard sirens.

"Now we're getting somewhere."

"Why are we hiding in here?" Mona asked. "It's just kids."

"It's a showdown," Nan said. "Don't worry about it. I know exactly what I'm doing."

She pictured the steam coming out of Pip Conti's ears when he heard, the slapping of his hands on the desk. For once in her life, Nan wasn't nervous. She felt like a train on a track barreling toward the station.

*

A SUSPICIOUS CALM fell over the next few days. Even the staff schedule had stabilized for once. Nan went about her business, knowing that Pip would strike back but hoping she had established a firm stance. She hated conflict, avoided it at all costs. Was this what she needed to change her life, though, to learn how to stand up when people tried to shove her down?

She set up the Hypochondria Hotline, met with the staff about the rules, and wrote the form that advised callers right off the bat that library staff were not giving medical advice and asked them to verbally agree so there was no confusion.

"Is this a joke?" Mona frowned suspiciously.

"It's meeting a real need," Nan explained. "People will call with a symptom, and we read them what their symptoms could indicate, right out of the medical books. Or what possible side effects their medication has. No different than if they were standing here and we open the book and show them the page. We're just reading it out loud, that's all."

"Oh, like story time for adults." Dunkan seemed to get it. That was a good sign.

"I like a good story as much as anyone." Trixie nodded agreeably. It was clear she had no idea what they were talking about, but at least she was amiable, bobbing along inside her own head.

Encouraged, Nan told them not to worry, that she'd handle the calls most of the time, especially while they were getting the new service off the ground.

"Good," Mona sniffed. "It sounds disgusting. I'd rather

not hear their nasty symptoms in my ear all day long."

Nan sighed. She'd hoped her great idea would be met with more enthusiasm, but no matter. When she was on the cover of *New Jersey Librarian*, Mona would be singing another tune.

CHAPTER THIRTEEN

"YOU LOOK HAPPY all the time," Nan said to T. It sounded like an accusation, but she meant it as wonderment. Who was this strange creature who came knocking on her door any time she felt like it? Why was she here in Nan's life? T was sprawled across her sofa, naked and eating grapes like a figure in a Roman bacchanal.

"What's not to be happy about? Especially at the moment." T grinned. She bounced a grape off her taut, hard-muscled stomach.

Show-off.

"How about right when you wake up in the morning. Are

you automatically happy for no reason?" Nan really wanted to know.

"Pretty much, aren't you?"

Nan didn't answer.

"You think too much," T said.

Nan looked at her, as self-satisfied as a cat rolling around on its back in a sunny spot.

"Is that so?" Nan was insulted. "Didn't you ever hear the saying that an unexamined life is not worth living?"

"You talk too much too."

Nan stood up. "Time to go."

"Don't be a sorehead," T said, laughing.

Nan didn't think any of this was funny. What had she gotten herself into? This whole thing with T was ridiculous, but she knew it was far from running its course. And she was definitely strapped in for the whole ride.

*

STILL RILED UP the next day, Nan was hoping for an easy day at work. But at the monthly library board meeting, the members would not look Nan in the eye. They squirmed in their seats, fussed with their agendas and pens, and generally appeared as if they wished they were anywhere else in the world.

Pip Conti had just revealed his master plan to have Nan run both libraries. He had ignored their first skirmish, when the police had to break up the middle school riot. Because he was wrong and had been outsmarted, she figured. That tactic had been between him and Nan; it hadn't worked, so now he was trying to get the whole board lined up against her.

Immaculata's advice rang in Nan's ears. She had to stand up to him, or her life would go swirling right down the drain.

"I need to inform you that this proposal is not workable or advisable," she said. "It would destroy public library service to the entire rest of the town, to the adults who are the taxpayers here."

She stood up, forcing the board members to look up at her. Her knees were shaking so she put her hand on the table to steady herself.

"Two different animals," she said. "The school librarian and the public librarian. Both require state licenses in completely different certifications. It's like asking a dentist to perform an appendectomy."

Chuck Hornfeck and Nefertiti Button nodded forcefully. They got it instantly, Nan saw.

"If my dentist tried to give me an appendectomy, I would

slap his hands away; I'll tell you that right now," Nefertiti said.

"This is all arranged," Pip said. "That's why the superintendent of schools is always head of the public library board, so the two libraries can work together. This isn't up for debate." He looked happy now that he had a real fight on his hands.

Nan stared at each board member around the table one by one, taking a long time before she spoke. "I don't want to."

Wow, that felt good.

"I mean, I simply cannot both run the public library and the school library at the same time. No one can. I will be glad to write you a lengthy report about why this is a terrible idea. That will give you a leg to stand on when you go back to the school budget and figure out where to find the funds to hire a certified school librarian. Which is not me. You hired me as a certified public librarian. If I'd wanted to work in a school and teach library classes all day, I would have gotten those credentials and would be doing that. Instead, I chose the lively fascinating world of public libraries, and I'm so happy you hired me to run this one."

The rest of the board focused their eyes on Nan. She felt like a mouse running around the room to avoid being swallowed whole by a python. *Don't look at me, help me out,* she pleaded with them silently.

"This is a direct order," Pip said.

She was furious. The meeting had started at a full boil and had now risen to a volcanic-sized eruption. She wanted to punch his smarmy face. She wanted to throw the biggest books in the library right at his fat head.

"I don't take orders," she said. "Deli clerks take orders. Soldiers take orders. Cops take orders. Librarians don't take orders."

She turned to the other board members. "I'll leave you to discuss this. Good night."

With that, she left the meeting and the building. Let them figure out how to close up and turn on the alarm. Let them knock Pip down a notch.

On her way home, she hid behind hedges and peach trees every time she heard a car or truck go by, in case they'd sent one of the board members after her. *This job has turned me odd*, she acknowledged. *I'm acting like I'm in a bad movie, where a private detective is following me.*

She finally darted out of hiding near her driveway, and then a motorcycle pulled over. It was T, dressed in full leathers. She pulled flowers from her saddlebag and handed them to Nan. Such an unexpected and simple gesture. She couldn't remember the last time she'd been given flowers.

"Get on," T said, pointing to her motorcycle and handing her a helmet.

"What am I going to do with these?" Nan asked, looking down at the flowers.

"We'll drop them off at your place."

"I've never done this before," Nan said.

"You're kidding. Where've you been?"

It was a smallish motorcycle, not a huge Harley Davidson or the like. But Nan was scared, excited scared.

"Only one thing to remember," T said. "Don't fight against it. When I lean, you lean."

"Lean," Nan repeated.

"And don't put your leg on the hot pipe; you'll get burned."

That's two things to worry about.

"I don't know about this." Nan hesitated.

"Get on, you goof. Do you think I'd give you a ride if you couldn't handle it?"

Nan wished she had one speck of the everyday confidence T had. What would it be like to live in the world without worrying, without running every worst-case scenario in front of you every minute?

She got on. She tucked the flowers inside her jacket. She leaned. She laughed out loud as they careened around the farm roads before they ended back up at Nan's apartment.

When she took off her jacket, the crushed flowers fell to the floor. Of course, they'd forgotten to drop them off before their wild ride. Of course, they stepped over them and went straight to the bedroom.

What a useless gesture, Nan thought the next morning when she swept them into the trash. They were flowers from T's deli anyway. Not special ones from the florist. What a lovely, useless affair this thing with T was, but what perfect timing she had. Nan could hardly remember what Pip had gone on about at the board meeting.

CHAPTER FOURTEEN

MR. EL. HE'S perfect for my secret book club. She knew the minute she saw him. He was a regular, often stopping after work at a local construction company, and on Saturdays, he'd bring his twelve children with him. A Black Jew, he was descended from a cluster of Black Philadelphians who had followed their rabbi to establish a community in South Jersey in the 1960s. Fifty years later, the community was thriving, with their own synagogue in an enclave they named Berakah (Blessing). He was her favorite library user. Every librarian had one, even if they didn't admit it.

Exceptionally short, Mr. El wore what looked like child-sized work clothes and tiny boots that were always mysteriously clean. Nan tried to picture him doing work that involved heavy tools and hard manual labor and failed. He must be a supervisor doing mainly paperwork.

She loved talking to him when he came in to pick up his many interlibrary loans from Ivy League university libraries and international libraries. The books were written in Arabic and Hebrew and French and mostly related to Judaism—to Talmudic studies, philosophy, and comparative religions.

He was not the rabbi, but he often served as study leader. The library staff agreed he was their most interesting library user. No one had ever met his wife, but she was probably interesting too.

"Can you imagine the dinner conversations at their house?" Nan asked. "Those kids are super smart."

The El kids had their library routine down pat. They'd march right up to the checkout desk every Saturday with a stack of books arranged facedown with the barcodes ready for the checkout machine, their individual library cards on top of the pile. The oldest went first, and Nan swore the rest of them lined up after her in order of age. Every single one of them thanked the assistant every single time. The assistants all loved waiting on the El kids.

"So many Els, they're in almost every class from kindergarten through high school. I don't know how Mrs. El does it, having a baby almost every year," Mona said. "Like the Catholics in the old days. My grandmother had fourteen; can you believe it?"

Nan envisioned growing up with twelve more sisters, twelve more Frannys and Reginas. Awash in sisters, what a horror show that would have been.

"I bet those El kids don't watch TV all night or have their eyes glued to their phones all the time," Mona added. "That's what's warping kids today, making them stupid."

"Stupid about a lot of things but smarter than we ever were about a lot of other things," Nan said.

Like sex. She'd learned about sex, at least the heterosexual kind, from library books. Anything written by Frank Yerby, with his lurid tales of tortured passion and revenge between enslaved women and their masters; D.H. Lawrence's *Lady Chatterley's Lover* (which she read in fifth grade), with its graphic descriptions of erect phalluses and women waiting to be plowed like fields, all in dialect so heavy she really had to work at it to know what the heck was going on; even her favorite life instruction manual, Betty Smith's *A Tree Grows in Brooklyn,* with its frank descriptions of extramarital sex, lurking pedophiles, and unwanted pregnancies.

When it came to lesbian sex, that was more of on-the-job training for her, starting at age sixteen in her junior year, with the captain of the high school girls' softball team. The few library books on the subject that she'd ferreted out—Rita Mae Brown's *Rubyfruit Jungle* and Isabel Miller's *Patience & Sarah*—helped though.

She had mixed feelings about the rainbow stickers used now on the library's young adult books. The stickers were supposed to lead LGBTQA+ teens and their friends to the books that would help them, but if they weren't brave enough to take those oh-so-obvious books out, how was that helping? If the queer books blended in with all the other young adult books, maybe they'd be taken out more. She lost sleep over that one. Maybe she would form a teen advisory group and ask them.

At least she kept her book selection up to the minute with LGBTQA+ books for kids and adults, plus all the others needed to meet demand—the vampire books, the graphic novels, the speculative fiction. Good god, those alone could take her whole budget. The people who read Harry Potter books over and over even as adults—she found it hard to understand why they didn't branch out eventually. But who was she to talk, she who read Barbara Pym novels over and over because she found new things to smile at every time?

Mr. El stood patiently in front of her.

"I'm so sorry," Nan said. "My mind was wandering all over town. What can I help you with?"

He handed her a slip of paper on which he'd noted a book title in his tiny block printing, as precise as an engineer. He never chatted, never made small talk. He was all business in such a polite focused way that she didn't take offense. It was a relief in fact; he was the only library user who didn't gossip or chatter on.

"I'd like to request this dissertation on Black Jews in Africa, but it's only available as a reference book in a library in London, not available for interlibrary loan," he explained.

He was also the only library user who regularly consulted the official worldwide library catalog even though it was free online and easy to use.

You're amazing, Mr. El. You are the ideal library user. You give my life meaning.

"It may also be available in digital form in a dissertation database," she said. "I'll be happy to find out for you."

She asked him to fill out the interlibrary loan form with all the information he had. She was dying to talk more to him about everything, anything. Where did he find these books he requested? How did they help him in his studies? Did he ever read anything for fun? She said none of these things. He was as far away behind his eyes as he could possibly be.

"Thank you very much," he said, turning to leave. "By the way, you're the best librarian we've ever had here. No disrespect to the others, of course."

"Of course," she said.

They thanked each other again in that ridiculous repetitive way people did when they wanted to say so much more but could only nod and bow.

That was her opening. She'd never get a better one. Leaning close, she spoke quietly, hoping no one else could hear.

"Mr. El, would you consider joining a book club that I am forming privately? It's more of a conversation than an obligation. Not reading the same book together but getting together to talk about what we're already reading. You are the most dedicated reader I know." She waited, afraid to hear him say that his life was so full of obligations a book club would be impossible for him. So many children, so much study and reading, so many synagogue meetings.

He bowed in a formal way and said he'd be delighted. While he wasn't a beaming or smiling kind of person, his eyes gleamed a little brighter. He handed her a business card, encouraged her to let him know when the club was meeting, and left quickly. A few minutes later, he came back.

"I forgot to pick up my interlibrary loan," he said. "What I came for."

He didn't say *Because I was excited*, but Nan felt his excitement in this little flurry of forgetfulness that was so unlike him. One little success for the day.

CHAPTER FIFTEEN

NAN COULD NOT resist T. When she heard that *tap tap* on her door, no matter how late it was, no matter what else she was doing, she felt compelled to open it. That mouth, that skin, that woman was delicious. She dove right in every time; she was all eagerness; she was drinking her in after a long drought; she was filling herself up on the feast of that woman.

She knew it wouldn't last. She didn't care. Who in their right mind would pass up immediate gratification at this excellent level? Honestly, she didn't even know if she wanted it to last. That thinking didn't apply here. There was no thinking when they were together.

They couldn't go to T's place because she lived with her grandmom, mom, and aunt.

"It's a big house," T said. "Huge, really. But they don't ever sleep. They're up all night. I can't relax there. I feel like they'd just be waiting for us to be done, and then they'd want us to watch a movie with them or play dominos, or they'd bring out all the food in the fridge and have a party. At least you have a separate entrance here."

I'm sleeping with a woman who still lives with her whole family. Nan laughed to herself. It was such an odd thought to think at fifty years old. Orphaned at fourteen, she'd lived with Franny and Regina, all of them banging around the house in separate states of grief and confusion until she left home at eighteen to go to college and never moved back.

"Do you like living with your family?" Nan asked.

"Love it," T said, sitting up. "They do my laundry; they make all my meals; they run errands for me."

"What do you have to do for them in return? Take them to their doctors?"

"Nah. They don't do doctors. They say don't look for trouble, or you'll find it. I don't have to do anything for them. That's the beauty of this deal."

"Nothing?" Nan couldn't believe how one-sided this

family arrangement was for T. But then again, one-sided relationships that were easy for T was what her whole life seemed to be all about.

"Well, I do supply them with news," T said. "I do tell them what people are talking about in town. But I'd do that anyway."

"It's a regular *Peyton Place* around here, from all the stories I hear at work." The latest story Nan had overheard was about the town baker who had walked in on her husband in bed with his high-school sweetheart. How the husband had to take the baker on the luxurious world-wide cruise she'd always wanted to go on to make up for his lapse. The part Nan loved best was that when the baker told the story, she laughed about it all and said she had lucked out to catch them together, so she could finally go on this wonderful trip of a lifetime.

Nan could tell by T's blank expression she'd never heard of *Peyton Place*, the salacious Grace Metalious novel she'd discovered as a teenager that made her realize many homes held big secrets and many women were not who they seemed to be. She honestly thought everyone knew what *Peyton Place* meant, even if they hadn't read the book or seen the movie.

"I don't know what you're talking about. As usual." T dismissed her.

So many things Nan and T said to each other whizzed right by without connecting. Their frames of reference were so different. She didn't know why exactly. *It's not like I was spouting metaphysical poetry from Andrew Marvell or something la-di-da.* She felt aggrieved, as if T had accused her of something rude.

It wasn't T's brain, education, or life experience; she had a business degree from Penn State and a minor in Italian language and culture, had spent her junior year abroad in Italy, and traveled all over Europe. But T reminded her of those kids she couldn't stand in grade school who had taunted Nan about her head always being stuck in a book. Like that was a bad thing.

I'm bored. The feeling bobbed up and poked Nan hard in the chest. But it felt really good to have such a strong, clear feeling. The words were a voice in her ear that she had never paid attention to in her other affairs and relationships with women. *I'm listening now.*

CHAPTER SIXTEEN

THE HYPOCHONDRIA HOTLINE was a burgeoning success. The phone rang often, people calling with the most fascinating ailments and symptoms. Lots of repeat customers—
Nan wasn't surprised about that. She knew all too well that
every day brought new symptoms to dedicated hypochondri-
acs such as herself, who woke up worrying about that cramp
in her leg being an embolism and went to sleep convinced she
might stop breathing in the night and never wake up again.

Nan created a spreadsheet to keep track of the questions
so she could report on the project. Maybe she'd be featured
in a national library magazine, leap right over the state library

magazine. That would be so cool, to be famous in Library-land.

The only problem was that Nan spent so much time reading symptoms and diagnoses in the initial rush of the service that her own hypochondria soared to an all-time high. Her stomach felt as if she'd swallowed a boulder. Not only that, everything near her stomach felt awful too—the top of her thighs, her lower back, even her sides. That was crazy. There were no organs in the sides of a body, were there?

She studied all the books on stomach problems. *Maybe it's my reproductive system acting up. Maybe it's mad that I never used it, so it's going to give me a hard time now.*

She whined about it to Immaculata, shocking herself. *The me who moved in here would never have told a landlady anything as personal as this.*

"It's gas, I bet," Immaculata said. "Just about everything wrong with us is usually gas."

"It's not gas. I never get gas," Nan said.

"Yeah, but you were never fifty before, were you? Skip a meal; you'll be fine. That's what I do. That, and suck on a lemon. The acid cancels out the acid."

"Lots of women with these exact symptoms end up diagnosed with a terrible disease," Nan said.

Immaculata shook her head. "Don't say it. You're asking for trouble if you say the word out loud."

"That's ridiculous. Saying a word out loud does not bring a disease on you." Nan wished she believed that herself.

"Your funeral."

Just in case, Nan refrained from even assigning any diagnosis to her symptoms. Over the next week, she skipped meals as often as she could without fainting, but it didn't help at all. She felt so full and uncomfortable, as though something massive was lodged inside her.

She tried all her hypochondria-fighting tricks: telling her body she was listening, that it didn't have to poke at her to make her pay attention; that she'd do whatever it was telling her to do, the minute she figured out what the hell was going on down there.

She tried distraction by reading thrillers and watching scary movies, but that never worked for long. She tried meditating to online videos guided by female voices, but it was hard to find a voice she could relax to, one without a strange chirpy tone or an unpleasant insistent joyfulness. She tried blunt-force realism, telling herself if she did have a terrible illness, she'd know soon enough.

She reviewed her hypochondriac history, the three

decades she'd spent fearing that the persistent twinge under her right arm was her death knell, when it was only her overreliance on using her right hand for everything, for never letting that strained muscle heal fully. All those years of worrying that the twinge was the C-word, all those wasted nights lying awake focused on that twinge and what it meant, dreading the treatment if she'd even get treated, which she probably wouldn't. When she finally got it checked out and they found nothing, she couldn't believe it.

It was always nothing, she told herself. It was nothing now. She tried to yank her mind away every time she thought about her stomach and this feeling that she'd swallowed a boulder.

She forced herself to walk home as usual. Main Street looked great at night, beautiful even. The old-style lamppost streetlights, the clean streets and sidewalks, the appealing store window displays. A long-haired calico cat trotted alongside her companionably.

Suddenly, she found herself soaring above the sidewalk, flying without ever deciding to fly or flapping her wings. She heard church bells pealing in the air above her and wondered if she had made that happen somehow. Then she landed hard on the hood of a huge black Cadillac and found herself peering in the windshield at an old man's head bent over the steering wheel. Nothing hurt, but she couldn't move. She struggled to understand what had happened to her. Her arms were pinned under her body, and her legs were hooked over the edge of the hood like a deer hit while trying to cross the road.

I'm roadkill. That was her last thought before she passed out.

*

IN THE EMERGENCY room, she was able to move her arms and legs, answer all the questions they asked her, and blink up at everyone who came in—an endless tide of radiologic technologists, nurses, doctors, and assistants, each with a specific purpose for a part of her body. One of her ribs was bruised, the medical chorus finally informed her. Nothing to do but let it heal. A few weeks, and she'd be totally fine.

She realized she'd never seen this coming; she'd neglected to worry about getting hit by a car. She'd worried about cancer; she'd worried about liver failure from drinking too much wine; she'd worried about every freckle and every bump on her skin turning lethal; she'd worried about her reproductive system taking revenge on her for not using it. But not this.

"Did the man who hit me die?" she asked.

"Iggy Ianucci? No, no, he's home already," a nurse explained.

"Did the cat die? He was walking me home."

The nurse looked skeptical, but she called someone named Gary and asked him before reporting back. "Gary was with the first ambulance crew and says he didn't see a dead cat. Was it your cat?"

Nan shook her head no. She was so relieved. The thought of the calico cat flattened beneath the black Cadillac was awful. She pictured the cat walking another woman home right then, and she felt better.

"What happened? I didn't see anything," Nan said.

The nurse hesitated, whispered. Her face was flushed and her mouth set in clenched disapproval. "I'm not really supposed to talk about it, but between you and me, that's his third accident this year. He runs that car right up on the sidewalk because he can't see out of one eye at all and the other one only a little bit. They fined him, took his license away last year, but he keeps finding the keys and taking off again. He's ninety-two. He's going to kill somebody the next time. I think they should lock him in jail and throw away the key, if his family can't keep him off the streets."

Nan felt like she'd won the lottery. She'd survived getting hit by a car. Hey, that was one death sentence she'd never even worried about. She'd worried so much about the boulder in her stomach and so many other ailments over her whole life—instead, she was the victim of a two-ton car aimed at her by a blind ancient.

This was cosmic proof that you never see your real death coming; it was always a surprise. If that didn't teach her not to worry, nothing would.

Everything felt different to her now. Her stomach felt normal, the boulder inside her rolled away. She still had time, she was ready, and her whole future life danced in front of her.

*

"GUESS WHAT?" NAN called both her sisters at the same time, she was so excited. That was rare. One at a time was usually the most she could handle.

"Is it something bad? Oh no." Franny the Fearful strikes again.

"Give us a clue." Regina could be the star of a *Name That Illness* TV show. She could name that disease in one symptom.

"I got hit by a car."

Nan heard a loud thump, like one or both of them had collapsed to the floor.

"It's fine," she continued. "I'm good. I didn't even get that hurt. Just a bruised rib. They don't even do anything for a bruised rib. They just send you on your way to live your precious life. Isn't that fantastic?"

"What's fantastic about it? You could have died," Franny said.

"You almost died," Regina said.

"I lived," Nan said. "The point is that I lived. I got hit by a huge car, thrown onto its hood, and survived with only a bruise."

For once, Regina and Franny were quiet. Nan didn't expect them to understand, really. All that mattered was she'd been given another chance, and she knew it.

The old Nan was a (*sorry to say this, but self, you need to face it*) loser. She chased women as if she were a dog running after cars but with as little chance of catching them as the dog had. She'd fallen into her first job as if falling into a kiddie pool and stayed there for twenty-five years, splashing around and never learning how to swim laps like the grown-ups. She applied for random jobs based on their titles and locations as if she was picking horse race winners by their cute names, not by their record or chance of success.

She didn't know who her new self was exactly, but she most definitely knew her first step. She had to delete the letter T from her alphabet.

CHAPTER SEVENTEEN

THIS IS HOW life is. When you decide to do something, the universe ties a bow on it and presents it to you to help out.

T roared by Nan on her motorcycle. A woman was clinging to T's back exactly as Nan had. She couldn't believe it when she saw who it was. It was unmistakable though. Lolly Fizzarella. The married (to a man) Lolly, mother of a brood of six children. The story in town was that during the last birth she'd sat up on the delivery table and pulled the baby out by herself with a roar, this superwoman who ran marathons and went on mountain climbing trips for fun.

Maybe they're just friends, Nan reasoned with herself.

But even as she tried to convince herself, she knew it wasn't true. The many failed relationships in her past had given her a pretty good radar for types. T was a true hit-and-run lover, showing up when she wanted sex. It made an odd kind of sense that she'd have other women on the ready, ever the opportunist. She clearly wasn't interested in any kind of commitment or regular dating. Nan didn't even have her phone number.

The town's only motel was at the end of the farm road where it met the highway. That was where the two of them were clearly headed, to the adultery motel with hourly rates. *That's what you have to do when you mess with married women in a small town.*

Seeing Lolly and T together cinched Nan's decision. Living with Immaculata and Joe, hearing their burbling laughter and bits of their conversations float up to her at all hours, seeing them hold hands while sitting on their garden bench watching the sunset, made her long for more than a tap on the door and excellent sex once in a while. It might not sound like something a self-respecting, independent feminist would say, but the truth was she really didn't want to end up old and alone like Marcia Ivory in Pym's *Quartet in Autumn*, who descended into madness and starved herself to death.

She deserved more. The only thing she had with T was chemistry; as fantastic as that was, it wasn't nearly enough. It was as simple as that. For once in her life, Nan wasn't going to talk herself into anything that wasn't right for her. She was sick of hoping that the woman she was seeing would change. There was no point to a life with someone she couldn't even talk to. She didn't survive a car crash to keep this limp excuse for a relationship going.

Nan made a pact with herself. She wouldn't spread it around that she'd seen T and Lolly together. She wouldn't lower herself to be such a gossip. And the next time T showed up, she'd pass. T was a fever that had peaked and faded away. That felt right and true.

*

A FEW DAYS later, Nan heard T before she saw her. That full-throated growl of her motorcycle as it crept up behind her, the crunch of the gravel as T stopped by the side of the road. Nan turned around to see T pulling off her helmet and sliding off the bike.

"Hey, babe. Hop on. I was headed your way." T held out her hand.

No time like the present. Nan knew what she had to do.

She had to be honest with herself and another woman, maybe for the very first time in her life.

"No thanks."

"Come on. You don't want to pass this up." T actually had the nerve to point to her crotch.

Ewwww. The needle on the crude-o-meter hits the highest point possible. Aaaaaanndddd I'm done.

Nan was reminded of awkward marriage proposals in Barbara Pym novels, where the women made fun of the men afterward to their friends, imitating the way the men had assumed they'd be thrilled when the women actually were struggling not to laugh and figuring out how to reject them kindly.

"You are delicious, T. But I don't need midnight snacks. I need breakfast, lunch, and dinner too. You know what I mean?"

T winced. Nan saw she'd landed a blow unintentionally.

"You want it all," T said.

"Not just leftovers." Nan pictured Lolly and all the other women T had undoubtedly enjoyed in passing.

"But not all leftovers are bad. Take day-old bread," T said. "It's really, really good the second time around, toasted, rubbed all over with garlic, and then dripped with warm olive oil."

Nan didn't know whether to laugh or barf. This woman would flirt on her deathbed.

"Bye, T. It's been fun." If Nan hadn't been sure before about ditching T, that image of day-old bread clinched it. She preferred fresh. And she was never going to find a real love if she would settle for this lame affair. Time to move on.

*

NAN'S RIB THROBBED. Every breath she took hurt as if a tiny evil sprite was inside poking her. She watched a very old man using a cane struggle up the library's front steps, bent over at an angle that looked impossible for him to stay upright. She rushed over to the door and held it open for him. He looked annoyed.

"My daughter made me come," he said, pointing to a black Cadillac idling by the curb.

Nan waited. Something about the whole encounter felt familiar to her. Had she waited on him? Was there a book she was supposed to find for him?

"Ever since I hit you, they won't let me drive anymore. I'm on house arrest at my daughter's. I hate it. I want to drive. But I am sorry I hit you," he said, turning to leave.

Iggy Ianucci. Apologizing for giving her another chance.

A chance to stop worrying about things that would never happen. A chance to ditch a woman who was not right for her instead of wasting years she didn't have, hoping it would work out. A chance to shift out of survival mode into full dancing-in-the-streets happy mode. She wanted to kiss the old guy.

"I forgive you, Mr. Ianucci. You gave me quite a jolt, but I'm doing great now." She meant it.

He sighed and struggled back down the steps. It was excruciating to watch him, hunched over, mostly blind, trying to feel his way down the steep concrete steps. Why didn't he use the handicapped entrance around back?

She knew why though. It was a slow laborious process to get in. First, they had to ring a bell and wait for a staff member to let them in. Then, they were in the Children's Room in the basement and had to wait for the elevator to be unlocked so they could get up to the first floor. If the elevator was even working that day, always a crapshoot.

How ridiculous it was to have a Children's Room in a former jail cell in a basement, where bad things happened when unsupervised, and how impossible it was to keep it supervised. How laborious it was for people with canes, wheelchairs, walkers, and baby strollers to get in and out of this library.

This town needed a brand-new library. Desperately.

Instantly, Nan could see it gleaming before her: A light-filled, glass-front, one-story building, spread out over a whole town block like a woman flinging her arms out in welcome. A sliding front door so smart that it knew when someone was standing in front of it with an armload of books to return or a wriggling toddler, or leaning on a walker decorated with flowers and tennis ball caps, or rolling up in a wheelchair.

There was really no reason why not. It wasn't as though this was a classic Carnegie building, those gorgeous jewels of libraries that deserved historic preservation. This was a concrete-block monstrosity, built to be a jail.

Nan bet someone with a big mouth, courage, persistence, and innovative ideas effortlessly coming out of her ears could make a new library a reality. Realistically, she knew it would be as difficult a task to accomplish as climbing a mountain or circumnavigating the globe. Money was always given as the reason, but that was just a convenient excuse meant to keep things at status quo, limping along. Funny, though, how politicians always found money for projects they wanted.

An icy, distinct thought chilled her. Maybe she was supposed to take this on. Maybe this was what was up ahead for her life.

Nah. Who was she kidding? She was the woman who held the record for being the most lackluster librarian of all time, with twenty-five years of doing nothing much in her profession.

Until now. That was the old Nan. Was the new Nan up for the challenge of a lifetime? At least a big project would take her mind off her love life; that would be a plus. She felt a mix of dread and exhilaration; what a most curious swirling energy.

Crazy idea. She put it aside, mentally shelving it to a dark corner. After all, she was the woman who had presented the library budget to the town council while sweat ran down her face from nerves. Which they'd immediately slashed up like a revengeful lover in a psychological thriller ripping up clothes with a butcher knife.

Back to your library/jail was their clear message. No change. We'll stick to the way it's always been around here. That was good enough for you.

CHAPTER EIGHTEEN

THE THREE OF them—Mr. El (she still couldn't call him Benjamin, he'd always be Mr. El to her), Chuck, and Nan—met with Nan at the coffee shop across from the hardware store for the first meeting of the secret book club. The men were quiet at first and kept looking at Nan to run the meeting.

"To be clear," she said. "I'm not in charge here. This is informal, a conversation about what we're reading. I'll start, but please jump in anytime."

She was reading a huge novel, one that, because of its sheer size, no book club in its right mind would try to get members to read: *Ducks, Newburyport* by Lucy Ellman.

"Can you imagine a book that is over a thousand pages long and mostly consists of one long sentence, an inner monologue? Can you imagine that the thoughts of a pie-maker with a husband, four children, and a flock of backyard chickens can be so fascinating and involving that you look forward to picking it up every single day and don't want it to end? Here's how much I love this book," she said. "I love this book so much that I don't read it while I'm eating."

Mr. El's eyes widened. "When I love a book, I push away from the table, wash my hands, and only touch the book with my clean hands, sitting in my special reading chair."

"When I love a book," Chuck said, "I carry it around with me just to feel it on my body. Even after I'm done reading it, I keep carrying it with me so I can touch it."

This is going to work out fine. These are my people.

After they'd talked for a long wonderful while about the books they were reading, Nan shared the troubling messages someone had been leaving her in the book stacks. The latest, found piled on a seat by the back door, read:

Forever is a Long Time

Forget Me Not

My Name is Anonymous

"I'm going a bit crazy, trying everything I can think of to catch the person who's asking for help. I skulk around the library like Nancy Drew, Girl Detective, but I can't catch anyone doing it."

"Are you meant to?" Mr. El asked. "Perhaps you are meant to be the receiver of the messages, and that is all. Perhaps the person needs to say these things but can't say them out loud. Perhaps you are helping by merely providing the forum. Perhaps that is sufficient."

"You may not be able to fix this. Trust me, it's the hardest thing in the world to accept what you cannot control," Chuck said. "My only daughter, our beloved Kennedy, has a drug problem. She dropped out of college last semester, and we don't know where she is."

One tear rolled down his cheek. Nan reached out and put her hand over his.

"Sitting still, sending out your own peaceful messages to the universe to say, I'm here for you, come and find me when you want help," Chuck continued. "It's a hell of a way to live, but there you have it."

He seemed so lost in his own thoughts.

"Comfort books," she said. "What do you read when you need comfort? For me, it's Barbara Pym, that genius British novelist who knew how to make every single word count. I read her books over and over, each time finding a laugh in a new place, or an insight that I now understand because I have gotten to the time in life that she's describing with so much humor, love, and grace."

Mr. El looked a little sheepish. "*Wind in the Willows* by Kenneth Grahame," he said softly. "It's not really a children's book. I reread it every year and linger over it. So wise, so funny, so very beautiful."

"For me, it's Mary Oliver's poetry," Chuck said. "She knows what life is, what pain is. She finds beauty everywhere; she finds peace outside. She reminds me that I can go on, that pain isn't unique to me, that this is what the human condition is all about. I am human, that's all. This is being a human."

He reached out and patted both of them on the arm. "My friends, tonight has been wonderful. Thank you. My heart is full."

"So many teachers are in books," Mr. El said. "So many souls reaching out to our souls over so many millennia."

To Nan, Mr. El said, "You are practicing a most noble profession. What an honor to be in the world of libraries. What a legacy to contribute to."

That vision of a shiny, big, new town library shimmered

before her again. But she said nothing. She did not have the faintest idea of how to move forward toward it. But she loved thinking about it. That was enough for today.

CHAPTER NINETEEN

JOE AND IMMACULATA on one side of the dinner table, Nan and Jeremy on the other. *What a queer little family I've found.* Nan laughed to herself as she passed the braciola and polenta.

Jeremy wrinkled his forehead at the unfamiliar dish, but he loaded up his plate anyway. He'd shot up an inch, and his whole body had plumped up since Immaculata had started feeding him. At first, he'd shaken his head no when Nan handed him bags full of Immaculata's food, but when Nan told him he had to eat it all or else he'd have to leave the library, he'd inhaled it and never objected again. She had set up a corner of the meeting room for him to eat in private every day. He never left a speck uneaten.

"What is this, Immaculata?" Nan wasn't sure herself, but she knew it would be amazing. Everything this woman made was delicious.

"Where you been? You never had this?"

"I lived on potato chips and pizza before I met you," Nan said.

"It's just beef, sliced real thin, rolled up, stuffed with bread crumbs and cheese, then fried. And the yellow stuff is cornmeal mush."

"I didn't know mush was food." Jeremy widened his eyes in surprise. "I thought it was a command to sled dogs to make them go faster. Like in the Iditarod Trail Race in Alaska."

"Where'd you learn that?" Immaculata asked. "You're a smart one, aren't you?"

"I read a great book about the race. I want to go see it someday," Jeremy said.

If it wasn't for the library giving this kid ideas of bigger ways to live his life, where would he be? Nan loved picturing him in Alaska.

"I bet I know something you both don't know," Immaculata said. "Did you know we got a lot of millionaires in this town?"

"No way," Nan said.

This was not a flashy town. It was a workaday town, where people kept on using furniture from their parents' and grand-parents' houses, so old it sometimes came back into style. It was a town where tools the previous generations had used were still oiled up and hanging, ready for use, in sheds and garages. It was a town where ancient tractors and pickup trucks creaked and bounced along farm roads.

"Joe will tell you. Tell her, Joe."

"We got a lot of millionaires in this town," Joe repeated, nodding.

"From what?" Nan asked. "There's nothing here."

"Way back when, there was a ton of money made from rumrunning during Prohibition around here. A lot of cash stashed and passed down," Immaculata said.

"Rumrunners—that would be a good name for a bar," Nan said.

"Not around here." Immaculata laughed. "These people like to pretend they got their money legit. Nobody talks about all the criminals in their family, not out loud, not in public. My dad had a boatload of money, but he was only a tailor. He didn't get all that from his shop; you better believe it. When his father and mother died, they found cash all over that house and a map to where the rest of it was buried. They didn't believe in banks. They didn't like paying taxes either. My dad was the same."

Joe smiled and nodded, clearly projecting *I love Sammy.* He tapped his head with his index finger to indicate what a smart guy Sammy had been.

"What's a rumrunner?" Jeremy asked.

"People who smuggled liquor on the rivers through the woods, back when alcohol was illegal for a while. That stupid law made a lot of families around here rich," Immaculata said.

Nan was fascinated to think of cash flowing through generations, a secret underground economy. "Hey, what do you think about a library program on rumrunners in South Jersey? I bet there's a historian who wrote a book about it. I bet people around here would love to hear more. Especially if they're related to a rumrunner or two."

Joe pointed his finger at her as if to say *You've got a winner.* Nan was starting to understand him even without words.

Jeremy asked, "What about a talk on the Jersey Devil too? It's so cool. As tall as a dragon, it's got a goat head and bat wings. There have been lots of sightings around here. I did a whole report on it."

Jeremy knows more about this town than I do. I better get on that.

"I know plenty of people who seen it. Not crazy people either," Immaculata said. "Like my brother-in-law Bobo—he was coming home way late at night one time on a back road in the woods. He had to put on his brakes fast when something crossed right in front of him. He couldn't make out what it was in the headlights, thought maybe a raccoon or a possum. Then it ran off, and then right away, another something crossed in front of him, bigger this time. He thought it was a fox, then something even bigger, a bear. The animals kept coming, running across the road like that for fifteen minutes. He watched it all from his car, a stampede, starting out with the small ones and then bigger and bigger until the last one. Bobo swears it was the Jersey Devil because it didn't look like any animal he'd ever seen. It walked on two feet, it was huge, and it had a swishy tail."

Nan loved ghost stories. This sounded like a wild demon animal and human monster mash-up to her.

Joe started to speak up, then hesitated.

"Tell them, Joe," Immaculata urged.

"I smelled it. In the woods. Middle of the night."

When they pressed him to say more, he shook his head.

But now, Nan was totally intrigued and excited. There couldn't be any town in the state with a more interesting history than this one.

"Awesome idea, Jeremy. I'm definitely going to have a library program on that," she decided instantly. She'd love to hear these stories from actual witnesses.

*

AT THE NEXT staff meeting, Nan asked them what they thought about hosting a local history speaker series, one on rumrunning and another on the Jersey Devil.

"Did you know the glass industry started here? Glassmaking was really big in South Jersey," Dunkan said. "My great-great-great-great-grandfather was a glassblower back in the 1800s. That would be a good topic too." He found a reference book on South Jersey glass factories and showed them a photo. "Whiskey flasks, that's what they made mostly." The flask, made of shimmering pale teal glass, had a pleasingly rounded shape, etched with a stunning weeping willow tree design.

"This is a work of art," Nan exclaimed. "People drank whisky out of these?"

Dunkan seemed to shine with pride at the compliment

as if he had personally blown the glass. She definitely wanted to encourage his ideas as she was starting to realize his quiet brilliance.

"Perfect," she said. "So how about a series: rumrunning, glassblowing, and for the headliner, the Jersey Devil. We'll make a big display of our local history books and movies and ask the newspaper to run feature articles. Maybe there's even a grant available to fund speakers' fees so we can pay experts and scholars to visit."

"I like rum," Trixie said dreamily. "They should make a drink called the Jersey Devil, with rum and hot sauce."

Nan shuddered at the thought of dopey Trixie as the guardian of the fragile life of a child. The woman couldn't stay on topic to save her life. Good luck, spawn of Trixie. You'll need it.

She had to admit though, that Trixie was a unifying force among the staff. It was always Everyone Against Trixie, which was undoubtedly a very good thing.

CHAPTER TWENTY

IT WAS THE best kind of day to be walking to work, Nan decided. Not too hot, not too cold, the sun on her face making her feel like only good things could happen today. Her rib didn't hurt too much, a little throb to remind her of how wonderful it was to still be in this body, in this beautiful world. She had left home early so she could dillydally.

She watched a pair of cardinals hop from branch to branch on a dogwood tree in full pink bloom. They seemed to live there; she saw them almost every day. She swore they cocked their heads and looked at her like they recognized her now.

The breeze lifted the hair from Nan's neck like a caress and tickled the hair on her legs which she didn't shave, to make a statement: *I am not the usual kind of woman in this town. I am not straight. I am not well-groomed. I am my own special self.*

It was May. She had survived a crash. She had fun programs to organize. She could smile at dogs, babies, the old guys in front of the VFW Hall playing cards, and the road workers not even pretending to dig, just leaning on their shovels and shooting the breeze. It didn't mean anything, her smile. It was the euphoria of spring reminding Nan that her body was a marvel, and her life was a trampoline of pleasure.

When she got to work, their student worker, Amo, was waiting to talk to her by the front desk. That was unusual. He was a silent efficient machine, usually gliding around the library, shelving books so fast that he made it look easy.

"Remember when those kids screamed bad words into the library?" Amo leaned in to ask, his eyes locked on hers.

Nan had forgotten all about them. "Now I remember. That was a ridiculous way to start a new job."

"They're sorry," he said. "Somebody dared them to do it. They were just being little jerks."

"You know those kids?"

"No, I know *of* them. I heard about it," he said. "I just thought you'd like to know."

She wondered if it was one of his siblings or two of them, neighbor kids, or his cousins. This place was a hotbed of connections, pointless to figure out.

"Who cares now? If they're sorry, they're sorry," she said.

"One of them is on the honor roll now," Amo said proudly. "The other one, almost."

From foul-mouthed jerks to A students, now that is a transformation.

"They're not bad kids, is all," Amo said softly.

It was important to him that Nan knew. That was obvious. Suddenly, the story became a funny one to her, one that she could tell about her first days at work. That felt better than it had at the time, when she could taste her own fear in her mouth and picture herself being fired over it. She came, she saw, she conquered. The tomato hurling, conceived in desperation, had turned out to be the perfect response. Kids always backed down when they saw someone as wild as they were coming back at them.

She thanked him, then changed the subject to his incredible accuracy rate in shelving books. She wanted him to teach his methods to the next student worker they hired because Amo was headed off to university in the fall on a full scholarship. How in the world did he get it right instantly, every time, that 625.49203 came before 625.4991? With the numbers strung out like that, most people immediately lost focus and couldn't figure out which one came first.

"I don't think about it," he confessed. "If I think about it, I can't do it."

Like happiness, Nan realized. It has to sneak in a door left open a crack, it has to pop up from the subconscious.

*

"MR. CONTI IS here to see you," Mona said. "In your office."

So much for her happy day. It was too late for Nan to run. He was sitting in her chair, staring right at her. She took a minute, pretending to look down at her clipboard but actually reciting a litany of encouragement to herself: *You are tough. You are a mighty force. You are a badass librarian.*

She plotted a quick strategy: *Let him talk. You listen. Don't make any promises. Don't apologize. Don't react. Whatever he threatens, whatever he proposes, you say nothing. You're a permanent town employee. If he fires you, you have the rest of the board who will take your side. If he fires you, you can sue the town.*

She took a deep breath and walked in. The front desk staff were all frozen into position, so they could listen even though Pip got up and closed the door, standing in front of it with his arms crossed.

"I am not a man who backs down," he said quietly.

Nan nodded and said nothing.

"I lead," he said. "Others follow."

She waited.

"So let's straighten out this middle school library thing," he said. "I'm here to tell you that we've started the process to hire a certified school librarian next fall."

Nan was so startled that she shook her head like a dog with water in its ears. Had she heard that right? This was backing down on an epic scale. She could almost hear the *beepbeepbeep* of the world's biggest tractor-trailer reversing toward her, with Pip in the driver's seat.

"You came here to tell me I was right?" she asked. "How gracious of you." She felt like doing a victory lap holding her arms over her head like a boxer after a knock-out win.

"No," he said. "Let me be clear. It was my idea all along. From the very beginning. To help bolster our reading scores, I have always been a cheerleader for a strong school library run by a qualified professional school librarian."

Nan pictured Pip in a cheerleader skirt, holding pom-poms and running into the school library shaking them.

"Your idea," she repeated.

"Yes, it was my idea all along," he said. "Do you understand? You agreed with my idea, but it was all mine from day one. You went along with my idea, right?"

Nan understood then that he needed to save face; he needed to play the big man. He needed her to keep quiet and play along. She made herself stare at him for as long as she could without laughing. What an ego. What an asinine excuse for a person.

"You're a genius," she said. "Congratulations on your brilliant decision. I totally agree with your wonderful idea."

His lips twitched. Was that a smile?

"Now, why don't we conclude this meeting so you can go make more of your amazing ideas come true." Nan opened the door and held it out for him.

She watched him shaking hands with library regulars on his way out. Was that all it took to make this man happy? It was so little, in the scheme of things. She felt like she was the big winner here. It was time to seize her advantage.

*

"WE DESPERATELY NEED new books in many areas," Nan explained to the library board. "But we have absolutely no room for them. So my next big project is a vigorous weeding program."

Now that she had Pip Conti on the ropes, Nan had decided to press on with an urgent project. The local history series would have to wait for a bit.

A big new library was a pipe dream in the hazy, far-off future, but those blasted, overcrowded shelves were an actual emergency. The building would burst at this rate. She introduced the idea to the library board first.

The board members looked blank. She really couldn't expect them to understand even though they'd all been on the library board for years and had gotten annual training from the state library on their responsibilities as board members. Lots of things in life didn't sink in very deep until you needed them.

"It's like weeding a garden. You need to thin it out, and you need to move books along in a library."

Now they looked downright uncomfortable.

"You mean throw books away?" Sissy asked, frowning.

"Books that the town paid for?"

"No, no, weeding is discarding, but we follow the national library association guidelines all the way. We select books with outdated information like medical and science books, then we pull them out of the collection and move them along."

"Where to, the basement storage room? There's no room there either," Sissy said.

"If they're outdated, there's no point in storing them. That would be like keeping food that's gone bad."

The board stared at her in seeming disbelief.

What? You all keep food that's gone bad?

"We'll have a huge book sale," Nan proposed. "The Friends of the Library group will run it, and everybody in town can come. I'll get Lolly Fizzarella and her crew to run it. Invite book dealers, owners of used bookstores too. They like to come to library sales."

"This is unprecedented," Pip said. "It doesn't sound legal or necessary." He didn't sound like his usual bombastic self though. He was definitely going through the motions. She narrowed her eyes at him to show that she knew. Her best librarian stink eye, that always did the trick.

"I'll be happy to show you the documentation," Nan said,

trying to sound firm but not confrontational. After all, she and Pip had made a private truce. Not that she expected him to strew flowers in her path in front of the others.

"This is standard library practice, happening all over the country in all kinds of libraries for many years," she explained.

"We'll look at the documentation and then decide," Pip offered.

It's not up to you. It's up to me.

"Or we could build a massive new library and keep every book the library ever purchased, even though no one wants to read them, and their dust and mold would taint everything around them," Nan snapped.

The way Pip reared back from the table, one would have thought a snake had bitten him on the ankle. Nan could clearly see what *he* thought about a new library.

To the others, she said, "You hire a professional because we are trained in our field. We go to graduate school to learn the law and practice of running a library. To be clear, this is not actually a board decision. I'm excited about our next phase, and I wanted to let you know about it. You can help spread the excitement. New books. *Brand new* books."

"We hire a professional because the state makes us," Pip said. "In order to get state aid, as I understand it."

You understand nothing, you bag of wind.

"All the years before I got here, did the previous librarians never move a book along?" Nan asked. "I'll give you examples of why we need to do this. Why we desperately need to do this."

She had a shelf full of ammunition waiting and pulled a book from the 300 section—the sex and relationship area. It was a marriage manual from the 1950s. She read, "To be a successful loving wife and mother is all the career any woman will ever need."

To their credit, Paul, Martin, and Chuck laughed out loud.

"I tell my wife that all the time. She laughs like she does at all my jokes," Paul said.

Nan brandished a book from the 900 section—geography. "This is a book on Africa where the Belgian Congo and Rhodesia still exist, where apartheid still exists in South Africa, where Mount Kilimanjaro's highest peak is still named Kaiser Wilhelm Peak instead of Uhuru Peak, which it was renamed in 1964."

They had the good sense to look ashamed. Nefertiti slapped the table and said, "Damn."

Nan waved one last book at them. "And here's a handy

guide to surviving an atomic bomb attack, from 1952."

Most of them laughed, but a few shook their heads.

Nan finished with a flourish. "Good people of the library board of trustees, we are guilty of criminal misinformation if we don't clean up our act. We have a duty to our residents. We can and will do better for our town."

Her voice rang out in the quiet room. This was the first time she'd ever used those words, *our town.* As if she were one of them. Was she?

When Chuck stood up and clapped, she smiled. When Sissy, Paul, and Nefertiti joined him, she waved a happy wave at them like she was a candidate for political office. They were on her team, she saw. She couldn't wait to get started.

*

NAN PRINTED OUT the weeding guidelines from the national library association and set aside time for a staff training. If they understood, if they were on the bandwagon, they would set the tone for the Friends of the Library group and library users.

"I'm sure you are tired of squeezing new books in between ancient books full of bad information, books that nobody looks at or uses," she said. "Are you ready for more space? For an easier job of shelving?"

"You should do this while we're closed," Mona said. "You're going to rile people up otherwise. They squeeze a nickel around here; they don't throw anything away."

"If you get anyone questioning you, you send them to me," Nan said. "This is how a well-run library operates. We're going to do this project while the library is open. We have nothing to hide."

Mona and Dunkan both looked startled as if to say, *Of course, we have lots to hide.*

"Didn't any of the other librarians discard books?" Nan asked. "They must have. This library has been around since the 1920s."

"They did it in secret," Mona said. "One at a time, little by little. When a section got so stuffed we couldn't squeeze one more in there."

Nan pictured a librarian smuggling old books out in the trunk of her car, driving deep into the Pine Barrens, and sinking them to the bottom of an unnamed lake weighted down with rocks.

"Well, we're doing this the right way," she said.

"That might be the end of you," Mona muttered. "You have to massage situations around here. You don't get too public about things."

"I do love a good massage," Trixie said.

They all ignored her. It was best not to engage in her flights of fancy.

"Well, we're a *public* library," Nan said. She thought the whole thing was ridiculous. Just let anyone try to give her trouble around doing her job the exact way the national library association said she should. It was collection management, and they'd hired her to be the manager.

She kept to herself the fact that the previous librarian hadn't been spending their whole state aid allotment every year. She hadn't stolen the money; she'd simply put the funds into the library bank account and left them there. That money was mandated to be spent every year, not hoarded.

But it had been too much trouble for her to work so hard, Nan guessed. That woman had one foot out the door for years before she finally left. The unexpended state aid was only to be spent on new books and materials; Nan had won a six-month extension from the state library to give her time for a big old buying spree. She felt giddy at the thought of all the new books that would soon be flooding in.

She weeded the first section herself, with the assistants watching her. She decided to start in the 500s, the science section, as it was one where the guidelines were very clear. If a book had a publication date over five years old, it was up for consideration for updating with a newer version because science changed rapidly, and no one wanted a student to submit a report based on inaccurate facts and outdated theories.

She opened a book on volcanos in the earth sciences area, checked the publication date (1979) and the index.

"Oh, look, in this book Mount Saint Helens hasn't erupted," she said. "Because it's still 1979 inside. I rest my case."

She moved the book to the empty book cart that was waiting to be filled with books to be discarded and replaced. It made a satisfying clunk when she plopped it down. She moved to the environmental area and pulled books with no mention of global warming, finding ten predating the current crisis.

"Look, a world without global climate change," she said. "Wouldn't that be a lovely thing, if it were real."

She felt a shift in the assistants as they relaxed behind her. They were getting the hang of it, she realized. Lack of understanding caused most problems in life. All she had to do was help them understand.

By now, the 500 section was starting to breathe, with every book having enough space for readers to browse without tugging and pulling. No books were plopped on top sideways because there wasn't enough room for them to be shelved properly.

"But what about the pictures? Aren't they good for something? Those kids are always looking for graphics to copy for their reports." Mona always had to say something. Nan thought she liked to hear herself talk, make herself big in front of the other assistants.

"Too old is no good," Dunkan said. "I show them how to get graphics out of the science database, not here."

Oh, now we're going to have a fight. It had all been going so well.

"Everything's not on the computer," Mona said. "Plus, the computers are busy all the time anyway. Sometimes you need a book, that's all I'm saying."

"We're going to get all new books," Nan assured her. "For adults and children both. I agree we need books. Wait till you see the beautiful new books we put in here. And they will fit once we make room for them."

Mona sniffed. "Why don't you buy them first so we don't have big holes in the section?"

"I'm in the process of buying them now," Nan said. "We'll do both processes at the same time—weed and replace, weed and replace."

She was exhausted. These people would be the death of her. She was even starting to have a little sympathy for the previous librarian. Maybe she hadn't been lazy. Maybe she'd been worn out trying to keep the peace.

"I need to sit down," Nan said. "Let's take a break."

While she was in her office, she heard Mona boasting to one of the regulars.

"We've got a bunch of new books coming in; wait till you see them. All the stuff you like, books on volcanos and climate change, and all that jazz. Brand new. I'll let you know when they get here so you can have the first crack at them."

She's not supposed to do that. Nan sighed. *We don't save books for our favorites.* Mona was supposed to have him place a hold on the new books and wait his turn if there were people ahead of him. But Nan wasn't going to fight two battles in one day. She felt a slight edge ahead, and that was enough for her today.

CHAPTER TWENTY-ONE

"I HAVE THIS itch on my left eyeball," Chuck said. "What does it mean?"

The guys now started out every meeting of the secret book club by teasing Nan.

"For myself, I am afraid that my large toenail is quite oddly colored," Mr. El chimed in, smiling. "Can you please help me?"

"You're ganging up on me." Nan grinned. "No fair."

They laughed delightedly. Obviously, they had planned poking fun at her Hypochondria Hotline.

"Seriously though, what kind of calls are you getting?"

Chuck asked.

"My first one was a gentleman with an uncontrollable urge to urinate at odd times," Nan said.

"What is an odd time to go?" Mr. El wondered. "Doesn't the body inform us correctly what it needs at all times?"

Nan thought about how her body had flung itself at T's body. She had to admit to being in great need of what T gave her. Sexual healing was real.

"The body informs us," Chuck said thoughtfully, "but is it correctly? For example, think about the times the body wants one thing, but the mind stops it. Are we ruled by our bodies or our minds?"

Who said philosophy had no place in daily life? Nan wanted to argue the case for the body ruling over the mind. She was sick of her mind.

"What books can you think of where the body was the ultimate winner over the mind?" she challenged them.

"How about *The Picture of Dorian Grey* by Oscar Wilde?" Chuck proposed. "His beautiful face and body stayed youthful for decades, masking the torment in his mind and soul."

They spent the rest of the hour happily discussing the

challenge, all of them taking notes on books the others suggested that touched on this question. *This book club is the
best thing I ever did for myself.* Nan congratulated herself.

If only she could make the rest of her life and work go as
smoothly as this. If only she could find out who was leaving
her such scary messages and help them. If only she could
meet the woman she was meant to be with for the rest of her
life. If only she could stop thinking like this, it sounded ridiculous, all this wanting and wishing.

*

JEREMY WAS HELPING Immaculata make pizzelles. She
still made them the old way, with a pizzelle iron, one at a time,
over the gas stove burner. Nan watched, fascinated.

"It's like magic," he said, watching Immaculata pour the
batter in, hold the iron over the flame, then pull the thin lace-
patterned cookie out.

"You're nuts," Immaculata said.

"Who thought this up?"

"It's not an invention. It's just a cookie."

"Can I have another one please?"

"Take that whole bag. Don't get sick on them."

This boy handled the bag of cookies as if it were made of

glass. This was a careful kid. This was a boy who was afraid of messing up. Nan wanted him to be carefree, a kid without a worry in the world. But that wasn't who he was. It was no use to wish people were different than they were. The way Immaculata accepted Joe; she said he was who he was and that was that.

They got into a rhythm of working—Jeremy mixing the batter and pouring it into the press, Immaculata holding it over the open flame until the exact moment of perfect doneness. It seemed to Nan as if the boy had always been by her side helping; it was that easy.

"Who are your people?" Immaculata asked.

"I only had a mom," he said. "But I haven't seen her in a long time. She used to write me cards, but now I think she can't find me anymore because they moved me to so many foster homes."

Nan and Immaculata exchanged looks over his head. Nan decided to keep quiet. Obviously, Jeremy would talk to Immaculata about things he wouldn't talk to others about.

"Joe don't have any family either," Immaculata said. "I got too many; he got none. You get what you get."

"I had a baby brother too," Jeremy said. "His name was Jakie. But they took him away, and he got adopted. Maybe they changed his name. Do you think they changed his name?"

"How the hell should I know? I don't know anything," Immaculata said. She put a dishtowel to her eyes and kept it there for a minute. Nan wondered if she were hiding tears. Her own tears threatened to spill out.

"When I go to college, I'm going to find him. After you turn eighteen, they have to tell you who your brother is," he said. "That's what I heard anyway."

What kind of a world do we live in, where brothers are kept apart until they grow up? And what had his mother done to lose custody of two children?

As if he read her mind, Jeremy said, "My mother didn't hurt us or do drugs or anything bad like that. She lost her job and then our apartment, and we were in shelters for a long time while she went to find another job. But she couldn't ever find one so they took us away until she could get one. But they never—they never—I never—she never—"

Immaculata slammed her pizzelle iron hard down on the stove.

"I'd like to beat the shit out of those people."

"Thank you," he said as if she'd given him a present.

"If it was up to me," she said, shaking her head.

"I'm going to be a lawyer. Because they can go to court and get things changed. Or a detective, they can find people."

He was quiet then, while he measured more ingredients into the bowl. Nan noticed how carefully he shook the measuring cup to make the flour settle down on the two-cup mark, put it on the counter, and bent down at eye level to make sure it was exactly right.

"Or a cook," Nan said, wanting to praise him. "You do that so perfectly."

He lit up, his face blushing to the tips of his ears.

"I love this kid," Immaculata told her. "Look how good he is."

Jeremy's smile took over his whole face.

The old woman and the boy were glowing, giving off such a buzz of warmth and joy that Nan put her arms around their shoulders to catch a little of it.

*

LATER, JEREMY LOOKED up from the front porch rocker and showed Nan his book, a beginner's guide to gardening. "I'm going to help Joe out back."

Nan sat down next to him. He was a sponge these days, reading voraciously and interested in everything.

"Did you know there's such a thing as a winter crop?" he asked. "Did you know you can plant things that deer don't like the taste of, so they leave your garden alone? Did you know some things you plant come back year after year, all by themselves? Did you know you can attract bees to your garden if you plant certain flowers?"

My god, Immaculata's turned him into a chatterbox.

Immaculata came out, laid her hand on Jeremy's shoulder, and smiled. "This kid, what a reader."

"College level." Nan praised Jeremy just to see him grin.

Jeremy followed Joe around like he was his apprentice. He held ladders and tools for Joe; he listened while Joe explained in few words what he was doing; he cleaned Joe's tools and put them carefully back when Joe was done using them.

"You know how to do everything," Jeremy said after watching Joe clean the gutters, freeing a long stream of pent-up stormwater that came rushing out of the downspout.

"Regular stuff," Joe said, smiling.

"Can you fix cars?"

"I can fix most things. But my best thing I can't do anymore." Joe showed Jeremy his knobby hands, his knuckles and joints swollen to double normal size, more like rocks piled up on one another than fingers and thumbs.

"I can't sew," he continued. "I was a tailor, but then I got arthritis bad. My hands don't go the way I need them to now. Sewing was my best thing. I miss it."

"But I thought only girls sewed," Jeremy blurted out.

"Sammy and me sewed. Immaculata's dad. We worked in his shop. We were good tailors."

"I never heard of a tailor."

"That's okay. You got a long life ahead to learn a lot of things," Joe said.

By then, Nan was upstairs with her door open, hearing the burbling of their voices. *That's what love sounds like. That's what happiness sounds like.*

She let that new knowledge flood over her and settle inside.

CHAPTER TWENTY-TWO

THE WEEDING PROJECT was a monster that had taken over the library. Nan needed help; she had to get rid of all the books she'd pulled off the shelves. She met with Lolly, glad to still feel a ping of admiration for the superwoman. Lolly exuded everything Nan wished she had: strength, vigor, confidence, joy. As long as they didn't share a woman, like a bad French farce—one coming in the front door as one left by the back door—this would work out fine.

"Oh geez, we haven't had a book sale for a really long time," Lolly said. "I'll have to look up how we do that."

"I don't mean to press you, Lolly, but I'm in a time

crunch here," Nan said. "How soon do you think you can get this ramped up?"

"You know me. I'm a fast, lean, running machine. But the others..." Lolly rolled her eyes.

Nan knew what she meant about the Friends of the Library members. Many were retirees; they were so booked up with traveling, dinner clubs, lunches out, gardening, babysitting, volunteering at the hospital, chair yoga, painting classes, and pickleball games that they were almost impossible to convene.

Lolly chirped reassurances that she'd get the group working on it as soon as possible. Nan believed her.

Jeremy wanted to help with the book sale. "I'm strong; I can lift the boxes. Can I be a volunteer?" He looked like a different boy now than the one she'd first met—a happier, round-cheeked boy with eyes that lit up when Nan talked about books with him. He'd been reading college admission and scholarship guides lately; she'd seen Amo bending over them with him. Library magic—that bringing together of people who needed to meet one another—shining through once again.

"No," Nan said. "I won't have volunteers here. We are a volunteer-less library. But you can help with the book sale."

"What's the difference?"

"Trust me. It's better for the library not to use that v-word. Remember Ms. Spitelli in your school library."

The middle school had a new professional librarian now—and he was an Air Force veteran, of all things. Johnny Button, Nefertiti's nephew. Suddenly all the boys thought reading was very cool. They even joined the book club Mr. Button started. Jeremy was the president of the club, of course.

He talked nonstop about him to anyone who would listen: what Mr. Button read (travel, history, poetry); where Mr. Button went to college (online for undergrad while he was in the Air Force, then Chicago State University for his graduate degree); what Mr. Button ate (vegan); why was he a school librarian (so he could have summers off); his favorite country to visit (Iceland, the Land of Fire and Ice).

We can't all be as glamorous as that Johnny-come-lately. Nan sniffed to herself, a bit resentful.

While he chattered, Jeremy hauled boxes into the meeting room, sorted books into subject areas, and pulled out ones that looked too beat-up for anyone to want. He made signs on the computer and mounted them into sign holders.

Friends of the Library members unpacked a few boxes,

then gathered to chat at the side of the room.

As if the discarded library books were not enough, the Friends had conducted a book drive. When the boxes of donations were unpacked, they found hundreds of copies of James Patterson and Michael Crichton thrillers and E.L. James's erotic novel series, *Fifty Shades of Grey*. Danielle Steel, Nora Roberts, and John Grisham books piled up as tall as mountains. No one ever donated J.K. Rowling's Harry Potter books. They were gold apparently, to be passed down hand to hand if those generations ever got around to having children of their own.

After Jeremy had done most of the work, the sale commenced with Friends clustered around a table with a cigar box to hold cash and change. After much discussion, they'd settled on ten dollars for an entire grocery bag of books and had stockpiled a massive number of bags for people to pack the books in.

When the doors were flung open, Nan couldn't believe her eyes. There was a standing-room only crowd out there. It turned out the book sale not only attracted library users but a lot of other readers who were intimidated by library due dates and preferred to buy used books they didn't have to hurry though. Lolly managed the crowd like a pro, spotting logjams and clearing them out, directing the Friends where to refill tables, and generally whirling around like a boss.

It was so exciting to feel so many books flowing out into the town. Nan pictured a river of books after a dam was released, watching people fish around in boxes and holding up their trophy books when they found one they really wanted.

Cookbooks were the prizes people elbowed one another to grab. And children's books—almost every single one was snatched up. Anything to do with gardening and do-it-yourself repairs were very hot properties. Biographies, even of obscure historical figures, were surprisingly popular. All those trashy, fun bestsellers went home to people who would take them to the beach and lake and not worry about sand and water damage. Nan noticed Pip's wife bagging up quite a few erotic novels; good for her. *Whatever keeps a marriage fresh.*

At the end of the sale, the Friends of the Library left for happy hour at their favorite bar. Jeremy had picked out a grocery bag full of old adventure stories like his favorite, *Robinson Crusoe.* Nan told him the books (lots of Zane Grey novels—who knew those corny old Westerns were still around?) were his payment for helping out.

Two leftover piles were carefully stacked in the farthest corner on the floor, lying down sideways so Nan had to read the message by putting together the book titles:

Don't Abandon Me

The Tragedy of It All

Listen When I'm Talking to You

And

My Life

Among the Doomed

Not Worth It

Nan was seriously worried now. This was deliberate. She needed to find out who was leaving these dire messages and figure out how to help them.

CHAPTER TWENTY-THREE

"FIRST OF ALL, I feel faint all the time," the woman said. "I have a rash on my big toes, only on my big toes. My bowels are loose, and that is not like me. I am known for my firm stools. My throat feels weird, not scratchy, more like hot in there, like the gas burner on a low setting."

She sounded so cheerful Nan wondered if she was happy to have such symptoms. It was funny how much Nan could tell about a person from over the phone: what type of home they lived in (chaotic or quiet); if they were pet people (her favorite was the bird lady who called, trying to talk over the racket her parrots made); what kind of preparation they had made for a phone request (all ready with pen and pad or searching for pen and pad while yelling at pets and children); what kind of response there was to what Nan read (eager or agonized).

Nan read her the standard disclaimer and made the woman agree out loud that Nan was not giving her medical advice. She started to read what the symptoms could mean, her mind automatically translating what the woman said into which page to flip to. The woman cooed and um-hummed happily as Nan read.

Bored people would rather be sick than do something about their boredom, Nan realized. She could hear the thrill the woman was getting from her possible diagnoses. If she were in charge of training doctors, Nan would teach a course in recognizing bored and lonely people. She'd test doctors on their ability to read voices and faces that lit up when there was a possibility they were sick and needed someone to touch their forehead or palpate their uterus.

Touch is the great healer, it seems.

Don't think about T.

One of their regular callers was a man with fallen arches in his feet. He liked to hear the list of recommended treatments: ice, stretching, physical therapy, orthotic devices. After

Nan recited the list to him, he'd launch in.

"But the best thing is when my podiatrist handles my feet. I don't know what he's doing down there, but he's an expert, that's for sure. When he gets done with me, I'm like a baby going down for a nap. That guy, he's gifted with his hands," the caller said, sounding like a man in love.

He needed the regular touching in that most sensitive of places, his naked feet, Nan realized. She let him go on for a minute, and then she'd gently detach and end the call. It wasn't quite soft porn, this foot handling, but close enough. Maybe this hotline wasn't such a hot idea after all.

Ever since the accident, her brain had been sending her clear and insistent knowledge like this one. Roadkill Nan had not been able to tell a bad idea from a good one. But now she could. And she was paying attention too, not just swatting things away she didn't want to deal with.

*

NAN NOTICED A teenaged girl camped out in the adult fiction section almost every day. *You're here so much. Are you the one leaving me message books?*

She reminded Nan of a piece of taffy that had been pulled to stretch out, her long bony legs not matching up with the length of her arms. Her glasses were too big for her face. Her hair was too much for her head, a wild mess of waves she'd tried to get into a ponytail without much success. Nan guessed she was fourteen or so.

"That's Brandy D'Ambrosio," Mona informed her. Who had named this girl? She deserved a more serious name, with her reverence for books and her self-possessed gaze at the world around her. This girl projected intelligence, had an almost visible armor up against the nonsense that came with being a teenaged girl.

Brandy seemed to be methodically pulling out books in the adult fiction section. She didn't check out every book though. Nan was trying to figure out what she was after without asking her outright. It was none of her business; the girl deserved privacy and anonymity.

She often sat in an isolated chair in the fiction section with a stack of books and read from each before carefully sorting them into two smaller stacks. Nan took a chance one day, stopped, and smiled at her.

"Have you read this author before?" Nan asked. "I haven't. What do you think? I'm always looking for a recommendation."

"First time. I just started it." She stared up at Nan with a brash keep-back look.

Nan tried to send harmless benign nice-person vibes back at her. *Are you asking me for help?*

"I was just wondering what you thought of our selection of young adult books," Nan finally said.

It was unusual to see teenagers anywhere but with their heads stuck in that section. An amazing number of adults read those books regularly too.

"If I'm honest, it sucks. They're all about other worlds, fantasy worlds," Brandy said. "I only like reading about the real world."

Nan had been exactly that way, too, at her age. She'd always hunted for books that read to her like an instruction manual on life. Through novels, she learned that character flaws like being a liar or a mean person would eventually be punished. That doing the right thing always paid off at some point, though maybe not right away.

She had loved Francie in *A Tree Grows in Brooklyn*, who worked hard for so long to have a good life and who got there in the end. How she'd made mistakes. Once she even lied to get a doll, but it made her feel really bad so she never lied again. How in *Gone with the Wind*, Scarlet was the glamourous one who seemed to be winning, but actually, it was

Melanie Wilks with her sweet goodness who won in the end.

Nan had read to find the answer to what makes people happy. Surrounded by a silent father, a weepy mother, and timid sisters, she had been determined to be the first one in her family to be truly happy. And to find out what sex was all about. That was a bonus.

"I see," Nan said.

"Or they're books about totally messed up kids—suicidal, abused, bullied, anorexic, and stuff like that. I hate that; it's so depressing. I only read adult books."

Nan loved that she took pride in that, like people who announced *I never watch TV. I don't even own a TV.* Brandy had the same kind of attachment to her self-image as an adult fiction reader.

Don't condescend to her; don't congratulate her; she'll hate that.

"I hear you," Nan said finally, turning away.

There were so many characters who came into a public library, drawn like a magnet to its quiet space, the chance to be alone in public, the world of books to immerse in, the internet and Wi-Fi access to use privately, a warm place on a cold day and a cool place on a hot day, a place where no one could throw you out if you didn't cause trouble, where you could stay for hours and not have to buy anything.

How in the world would Nan ever be able to figure out who was sending her messages and what to do about it?

CHAPTER TWENTY-FOUR

"I CAN'T READ," Chuck confessed. "I try, but I'm just holding a book, and nothing is going in. My wife says, 'How can you read at a time like this?'"

Lately, the secret book club had been meeting at the diner on the highway, a little more out of the way than right in the middle of town.

Chuck's daughter, Kennedy, had resurfaced after being missing for months, gone to rehab, and promptly run away again the day she was released. They didn't know where she was or how she was supporting herself.

Nan marveled at how Mr. El, that quiet and unassuming

man, that murmurer, immediately seemed to swell up, his body taking on a different body language. She saw the prayer leader, the counselor in him emerge.

"We will pray for you now," he said, bowing his head. He reached for both of their hands and prayed silently. When he released their hands, Nan felt a lightening. She hoped Chuck felt it too.

"A reader will always be a reader," Mr. El said. "Do not fear, brother. Reading will return to you. For now, do the best you can to get through your days. Comfort your wife. That is all."

He went on to describe the poetry of Kabbalah, from the mystical area of Judaic studies, that he was reading. He closed his eyes and recited several lines, his voice purring and peaceful.

"This book, these poems, have made me look at the world around me through different eyes," he said. "Do you know what I mean?"

Nan jumped in. "There are poems I keep on my desk at work. I read and reread them and they help me see things differently. When things aren't going well at work, I read Marge Piercy's lines in the poem, *To Be of Use.* 'The pitcher cries for water to carry and a person for work that is real.'"

Dunkan popped into her mind then, the way he lumbered around the library so quietly, the way he looked hungry for something all the time, the searching in his eyes.

"This guy at work, he needs work that is real. I'm going to ask him if he'll start a fantasy worlds book club," Nan decided instantly.

"My daughter used to love those kind of books," Chuck said.

Nan and Mr. El nodded, smiling at him. It was good for him to say anything at all. It was good for him to remember his daughter as a reader. It was good for him to remember anything good.

*

"DUNKAN, YOU KNOW so much about fantasy and speculative fiction. You're our in-house expert," Nan said. "Would you consider setting up a library book club on the topic for us?"

"How would I do that?" He looked astonished, as if she'd asked him to go deep sea diving and bring back a mermaid.

Nan outlined the procedure she had in mind. She'd set up a meeting schedule. He would pick the titles ahead of time so she'd have time to buy extra copies to lend. She'd write the press release and publicize the club. He'd talk to readers about joining the club when they checked out fantasy, science fiction, dystopian fiction, and other books that would fit under the speculative fiction umbrella.

"I've never led anything before," he said. "What if I don't know how? What if nobody comes?"

"Good questions, Dunkan. Let me ask you a question. When you don't know things, how do you learn about them?"

"I read a book usually."

She waited.

"I could read a book on how to lead a book club," he said. "Then I'll let you know. Would that be okay?"

"Totally."

"I read a book on how to fix toilets," he said. "Our toilet wouldn't stop running. So I found a book here in the how-to section, went to the hardware store, showed them the picture of the parts I wanted, then I fixed the toilet."

"What a great story. I should use that for the library newsletter."

"But don't use my name. I don't want anyone to know our toilet was broken. It feels too personal. I don't overshare. I'm not one of those."

This was the most Nan had ever heard Dunkan talk

about himself.

"I could make you a woman in the newsletter story," she said. "No one would ever guess it was you."

He cracked a smile, the first Nan had ever seen on his face.

"I'll let you pick your female pseudonym for the story."

"My sister's name is Dunna. Not Donna. My parents like to spell our names different. They want us to be unique. That's why I'm Dunkan with a *k*. No one spells it right."

"Want me to use Dunna for the newsletter?"

"No, everyone would know it was me. Dunna is so not interested in toilets or home maintenance of any kind."

"What's her deal?"

"She's a data modeler."

Nan had no idea on earth what that was. It must have shown on her face.

"Computers," he said. "That's all she cares about. She only reads software manuals."

"I'm sorry for her."

"Let's call our toilet-fixer Gloriana," he proposed. "That sounds cool."

Dunkan, you never cease to amaze me. There was so much going on in his head, none of it ever shown by the lack of expression on his face, his downcast eyes, his silence.

She had the strong feeling his shell was softening, and the real Dunkan was starting to emerge. What a bonus that he loved the very kind of books she couldn't stand; they would make a good team. She wouldn't let herself dwell on the possibility that the fantasy worlds book club could crash and burn and send him back inside himself.

CHAPTER TWENTY-FIVE

THE LIBRARY LOOKED so inviting after the clean-out, without all those sad old books crammed into every inch. Nan walked around enjoying the sight, imagining the books breathing a sigh of relief.

How long would it be before the shelves were jam-packed again? If she were honest with herself, she knew it wouldn't be long. The book sale was a very temporary solution; it wouldn't help all the other space issues. After school, every single seat in the library was always full, and the checkout desk now often had lines, lines that wound around right into Nan's tiny office. There was absolutely no room for a self-checkout machine unless she hung it from the ceiling and hoped nobody tall bonked their head on it.

Nan rounded the corner, turning into the blind spot in the Reference Room where she'd thought about putting up one of those security mirrors. There, she saw Lolly from behind, unmistakable in her running tights and hoodie. Nan wanted to thank her for helping with the book sale, to share her joy in the clean shelves.

"Hey, Lolly," she called out.

Lolly whipped her head around, her hands covering something on the table. That was strange. For one thing, she'd been standing there, not moving like the human perpetual-motion machine she usually was, not laughing and talking as she did when plucking books for her children to read during their mandatory daily home reading hours.

Nan saw it then, a stack of books, books that didn't belong in the Reference Room.

"It's okay, Lolly," she said.

"I didn't mean anything," Lolly said. "I was just..."

"Can I see?"

Lolly moved her hands away from the books and sat down. Nan had been wondering if the woman even knew how to sit, so mystery solved. Nan sat beside her.

The books read:

Betrayed

The Life I Led Before

Going Going Gone

"You can tell me," Nan said. "No matter what. It's okay."
"I really can't."

Nan waited. Silence could be so full sometimes. She could practically feel the truth bumping against the surface of the silence. She could smell Lolly's distress leaking out of her skin. The town clock rang the time slowly; Nan timed her own breathing with each peal.

Finally, Lolly leaned close to Nan. "It's the oldest story in the book. He's got another woman, another whole family in the next town over. Our six kids were not enough for him, apparently. He's got three more with her."

Nan felt that blow. She closed her eyes for a second, absorbing the shock waves that came barreling at her from Lolly. She didn't say anything but nodded back at her.

"I didn't mean to upset you. The titles of those books would just leap out at me when I was in here. I'd pull them off the shelves. Leaving them like this felt like I told somebody. It was a release valve for a few minutes. But I haven't told anybody."

"Not even T?" Nan wondered if T was Lolly's revenge on her husband.

"That was nothing," Lolly said. "An angry, needy moment."

"You're entitled."

"See, I have a moment of weakness after great provocation. But he has a decade of deliberate deceit. His oldest kid over there is ten years old. The youngest is one month old. That's the whole story right there. It's in the numbers." A tear escaped from Lolly's eye and rolled down into her mouth. She got up, her head bowed like a contemplative, her face as still as a portrait.

"I really love that guy," she said. "He's my favorite person on earth. I always want to talk to him, tell him everything I'm thinking and doing. And you know what? He says he really loves me too. He says he loves both of us, all of us. So what am I supposed to do with that? I feel like I'm going to explode." She walked out slowly, touching the books she passed with her fingertips as if saying goodbye.

Nan picked up the stack of books and brought them over to the shelving carts behind the checkout desk, where Mona stood watching everything, hearing everything, watching Lolly leave empty-handed, eyeing the books that Nan was holding, her eyes meeting Nan's with understanding.

Then a miracle happened. Mona said nothing. Nan understood she wouldn't say anything, that they had achieved the impossible, an unspoken agreement. Now that Mona was a person with a pain she didn't want to discuss—her son's divorce—she could recognize pain walking by her.

CHAPTER TWENTY-SIX

YOU ARE GOING down, Hypochondria Hotline. A good time was had by all, but the party's over.

Nan studied the spreadsheet she'd created for the staff to use. It was total guesswork when she came up with the form. Beyond a total of how many calls per week, she hadn't known what to keep track of. Because she had been curious, she'd made a checklist of symptoms the staff could use to track why people were calling. They had a bet every week as to which symptom would get the most calls, and Nan gave out a small prize to whoever guessed right. She did suspect that Mona rigged the calls sometimes, so she could win by telling her friends and relatives to call and say they had vertigo or halitosis or whatever symptom she was betting would win that week.

Nan noticed a strange regular pattern—one call per week with the symptom of uncontrollable urination. That was very odd. Not one of the usual symptoms they got over and over again. (Diarrhea usually ran neck-and-neck with backache, edged out once in a while by groin pain or itchy rashes.)

"This came in the book drop," Trixie said, handing her a bulging envelope with *Librarian* written on it in shaky old-man printing in block letters. When Nan opened it, fifty-dollar bills came fluttering out, landing on her desk.

"I love it when that happens," Trixie exulted.

"When does that happen, Trixie? Are you in the habit of getting cash in the mail?" Nan rarely tried to make sense out of what Trixie said, but she really wanted to know.

"Well, sure."

Trixie apparently lived in an alternate universe. Or maybe her ex-boyfriend sent her cash for child support that way. For all Nan knew, he might be as wifty as Trixie.

Nan read the note that came with the cash: "For the children's books I ruined. I am sorry, but I have a medical condition of uncontrollable urination. It is even in the book of symptoms. I didn't mean to do it. Please use the money to buy new books for the children. Yours truly." The note was unsigned.

Nan ran out to the front desk, gathered the staff around her, and read the note out loud. They cheered; she raised her fist in triumph as if she'd won something.

"He confessed. It's all over. It wasn't bad kids," Nan said. "Nobody hates us that much."

"Bad plumbing," Dunkan said. "Like a leaking pipe. Bad plumbing can do a lot of damage."

"You can buy a lot of books on toilet training with all that cash," Mona joked.

They laughed so loudly that people reading looked up at them. They laughed so hard that Dunkan threw out his arms and knocked over the display books on the counter. They laughed so long that people coming in the door laughed with them because laughter is more contagious than chickenpox.

Nan loved ending the Hypochondria Hotline on that triumphant note, quitting while they were ahead. She concluded her report to the board with a positive twist, saying the library would wrap the service into its already effective consumer health information services. She quoted grateful users of the hotline because she wanted the board to know the library was in the very bedrooms and bathrooms of its users: "I sleep much better now, thanks to what you read me about rickets. My wife is happy about that." And Nan's favorite: "Every time I go to the toilet now, I know what I'm looking at because of the information you read me. Thank you."

The cash fluttering down on her desk felt like the clincher for her decision. That was strange; she didn't know what to make of that. But this money felt significant somehow, as if those fifty-dollar bills were omens of more money raining down on her.

What a ridiculous thought. She and money were not on close terms, like cranky relatives best kept at arm's length.

CHAPTER TWENTY-SEVEN

NAN HAD HER eye on Brandy D'Ambrosio and Amo Gonzalez. She'd seen the teenaged girl and the student worker whispering in the auto repair section, the most un-likely place for either of them to be, as neither had a car or a driver's license. Amo had even taken his earbuds all the way out, so this must be important. They had picked their corner well. There was no way Nan could creep up behind them to listen.

So she boldly walked close to them, clipboard in hand, a frown on her face as if she was trying to solve a difficult refer-ence question. She pulled out a book and ignored both of them. They looked up briefly, then resumed whispering. Sometimes it was to her advantage to be a fifty-year-old woman, the epitome of invisible and unimportant.

"I don't want to," Brandy insisted.

"I don't either," Amo said. "But I will if you will."

"I hate that stuff."

"It's not that bad."

"Why should I?"

"Because he's a good guy. We're just helping out for a while. Please."

Brandy sighed heavily. "Just for a little while."

"You might love it when you get used to it," Amo said.

"I won't."

Nan had no idea on earth what they were talking about. But when they walked up to the front desk, bent over a clipboard there, and signed their names, she knew.

Amo had talked Brandy into signing up for the fantasy worlds book club that Dunkan was starting just as soon as he had six people signed up. That was what Nan and Dunkan had agreed on. If the library had six people signed up and a few of them didn't show up, Dunkan could still hold the meeting. Nan had been keeping her eye on the list; it had stayed steady at four people for the last month.

So Amo and Brandy had just made the fantasy worlds book club a reality. Nan wondered if Dunkan would be happy or miserable at the news. It would help him spread his wings. That was for sure.

*

SHE DID NOT foresee costumes. Two large women seemed to be dressed as fireflies. A group of teenagers in feathered capes swooped in. Someone in a mask that reminded Nan of a hermit crab shell took a front row seat.

She did not envision an overflow crowd. Apparently, fantasy worlds aficionados did not believe in signing up for things ahead of time, but they certainly believed in showing up.

Dunkan wore a long blue velvet robe with a gold sash. Under a pointy coned hat, his face bloomed bright red as he called the meeting to order and began with a dramatic reading, a short passage from his favorite fantasy epic. Nan marveled at his courage and flair.

She didn't catch the author or title of the book he read from—and it didn't matter because she'd never read it—but she had to admit she was sucked in instantly. The power of storytelling was stronger than its subject matter. Changelings! Conjurers! Demons! Ancients! Celestials! Doppelgängers! All of them tearing across a fallen kingdom in a quest to save the world from disappearing into a vast sinkhole of oblivion placed there by an evil lord.

As she tiptoed away, secure in knowing Dunkan had the club well in hand, she saluted all oddballs and different sorts, herself included.

All are welcome here. All are embraced here. In a way, the public library was as fantastical a world as these imaginary ones.

CHAPTER TWENTY-EIGHT

JEREMY SAT STIFFLY upright, his face serious, notebook and pen arranged on the library meeting room table. He and Nan had ducked in there for privacy. As always, this kid was determined to ace any homework assignment. A career day interview was no different.

"First question. Did you always want to be a librarian?"

Should I be honest? Or give him acceptable answers for his teacher. She opted for honesty.

"I didn't always want to be a librarian. I just wanted to hang out in libraries forever. They were my safe place. When I realized with a huge shock during my senior year in college that I'd soon have to make a living, that's when I decided to get a graduate degree in librarianship and work as a librarian."

Was it my true desire or the only plan I could come up with at the time? Was it my life path or just one part of it? Nan had taken an aptitude test that seemed to imply she was headed for a career in fast food, which made library school look way more appealing.

Jeremy took notes by hand, old school. He was practicing to be a detective or lawyer. That was how they did it in movies. She waited.

"What advice do you have for anyone who is considering being a librarian?"

Marry someone who makes more money than you will. Wait, that wasn't fair. She could have made a little more if she'd worked harder, moved up the promotion ladder.

"Work in a library first. See if you like the pace, the atmosphere, the people. Try it out before you commit. Work in several kinds of libraries if you can—university, law, medical, public, archive—they are all very different. That's the best way."

"Last question. What do you like best about being a librarian?"

This should be an easy question. But it isn't. The actual

answer is I'm used to it. Nan was ashamed to say that out loud.

Finally, she produced a better answer for public consumption. "People thank me all day long. I help someone find their birth mother or get their first email account set up. Yes, even in the twenty-first century, lots of people still don't have email accounts until they need one. I find a poem that someone has been looking for since their childhood. I find sick people medical information so they can talk over options with their doctor. I help people apply for jobs. Last week, I helped a woman find a book to tell her kids that their dad is gay. She couldn't find the words and wanted something on their level to share with them. She cried with relief, would not stop thanking me. It's lovely to feel gratitude coming at you."

Jeremy looked up from his notebook, his eyes widened. "I never thanked you."

Nan's heart swelled. There was something so pure about this kid.

"You made me feel like I was worth something, I was smart, I was going to be somebody. Not just a foster nobody cares about. That's huge. I thank you." And then he stood up to shake her hand, like a grown man, like the beautiful-souled man he was on his way to becoming.

Tears plopped out and flowed right down her face. She felt like she was saying goodbye to something, but what, his childhood?

CHAPTER TWENTY-NINE

LOLLY TOOK HER place at the diner booth hesitantly. She looked different to Nan somehow. She wore jeans and flip-flops—that was it. No running tights, no top-of-the-line running shoes. Her hair was loose, no ponytail bobbing.

She looks humbled. Nan remembered the times in her own life when she'd been humbled; it had felt like ripping off a bandage, her feelings so raw and tender underneath. Those times were when Nan realized that every single platitude and cliché about life came from a real place, that those comforting thoughts were actually true. It *is* always darkest before the dawn. Cracks *are* how the light gets in. Nan didn't remark on

Lolly's changes. She just welcomed her to the secret book club. Chuck and Mr. El both stood and shook her hand.

"I've been reading nothing but biographies," Lolly said. "It's the funniest thing. I never read them before in my whole life."

They all waited, sipping coffee and keeping eye contact with Lolly.

"Mostly women, but not all," Lolly said.

The diner fell silent, one of those pauses that happened naturally even when a restaurant was full of people, when it seemed like everyone eating had taken a big bite at the same time and stopped talking to chew.

One of those odd thoughts popped into Nan's head, the answer to the reference question she had been asked earlier: How many diners are there in New Jersey? The answer was approximately 525—more than in any other state. They were the real treasures of the state, in her opinion. Forget beaches and casinos. She kept the fact to herself. Now was not the time to spew interesting trivia on the table.

"All these biographies are about people who had it way worse than me," Lolly said. "Women who faced every obstacle with so much courage. Women who made a real difference in the world. I'm starting to get it. I can't sit around feeling sorry for myself."

"Ah," Mr. El said. It wasn't even a word, but it seemed to charge up the atmosphere at the table.

"Biographies," Chuck said. "That's brilliant. Exactly what I needed to hear. I need to read biographies too. I need to read about people with courage and faith. My daughter's home, but I'm so afraid every day that she'll relapse. It's killing me."

"After every one that I read, I think hard about how I'm going to live my own life," Lolly said. "I asked my husband to stay with his other family for a while. My mom moved in to help with my kids. I need time to myself to figure out my life."

"Wouldn't it be wonderful if doctors and therapists prescribed books instead of drugs all the time?" Nan mused out loud.

"Oh, I'm taking drugs too," Lolly said.

Nan knew she'd fit right into the book club when they all laughed. At first, Lolly had just a little grin on her face, but then she broke right out into an actual open-mouthed snort. She was one of them now.

CHAPTER THIRTY

CELIBACY IS NOT my friend. I am sex-starved, worse than I've ever been in my entire life.

This sad fact was now apparent to Nan, but what the hell was she going to do about it?

The problem was, once she'd started having sex again—after five long years without it (Fie on that last poisonous relationship)—Nan's body felt absolutely entitled to it. Her switch had been turned to the ON position, and it was impossible to turn it off. She got constant urgent jabs from below at the oddest times.

Once, while compiling book circulation statistics for her

monthly board report (the most boring task in the world), her body acted up alarmingly. The numbers were satisfyingly high, but her torment was significantly higher. She had to keep jumping up, pacing around the building, climbing stairs for no reason, walking around the block, but nothing helped. Her staff looked at one another and raised their eyebrows at her restless antics.

Don't you dare ask what's wrong with me. This is a true don't-ask-don't-tell situation.

Desire was driving her crazy. Solo shenanigans were inadequate, so boring and ultimately unsatisfying. What she craved was not only the release but also the surprises that erupted when two bodies connected. It was amazing how much she dwelled on her lust. Did everyone? And why hadn't anyone told her that being post-menopausal was more fiery than being a teenager?

It seemed all the satisfied-looking older women she knew had conspired to keep this knowledge from her. She wished she had the nerve to spread the news to other women who were afraid of menopause about how much stronger her orgasms were and how completely excellent sex was now. When she could get it, at least.

She even had an orgasm while she was totally, deeply

asleep. Who knew that was even possible? She'd never read that in any book. An absolute, full-on, huge climax as if a ghost had visited her and her body had carried on without her somehow. Waking up shaken and sad, with no warm human next to her, she finally succumbed to the one avenue open to her.

She timed her call to Russo's to shortly before closing, hoping T would pick up. *Should I ask for a personal salami delivery?* She rejected joking around though. Why not be perfectly straightforward, ask for what you so desperately needed? So she did, her voice sounding strangely earnest. She made it clear this was a one-time deal, a sexual emergency.

T showed up minutes later. "You can't just call me like that." Her face was serious. This was important to her, Nan could see. She liked to be the one calling the shots, obviously.

"Why'd you come then?"

"Same reason I always do." T pulled her close. God, that woman knew exactly how to touch her.

Was this backsliding? It felt more significant somehow and definitely not only about T. She had no interest in seeing T again.

What Nan was feeling was a huge surge of pride in herself for figuring out what she needed and giving it to herself. A very new feeling for her. She'd need to practice that until she got very good at it. She wanted to feel this every day for the rest of her life.

CHAPTER THIRTY-ONE

ORGANIZING LIBRARY PROGRAMS for adults felt like throwing herself off the highest diving board into a cold pool. Nan had never tried to lure adults off their comfy couches, away from their TVs with its endless stream of entertainment. They would bring their kids and grandkids to the library for story time and summer reading club, but would they show up for programs for adults like the local history series Nan had put together?

She steeled herself against expecting too much. Especially after the debacle of the classic books lunchtime lecture series back in spring. She and the speaker sent from the state arts council had sat and eaten meatball sandwiches together in the empty library meeting room for three sad Wednesdays in a row. Classics remained the books everyone planned to read but never actually did, apparently. And never again would she use the word "lecture" to try to attract adults. That was the kiss of death, she now knew.

He was a very young adjunct professor from the nearby community college, so new to adult realities that she could almost see his rosy dreams glowing on his baby-doll cheeks. She could still hear the awful sound of their gummy chewing in the silence and picture the way he had looked up hopefully at every distant sound and down again sadly when the door stayed closed. It broke her heart; she'd tried so hard to get people to come talk about the great books, and no one had, those jerks. Mona had the nerve to say, "I told you so," right to Nan's face. It only made Nan more determined.

Before the rumrunning program, Nan gave an interview for the local newspaper and even appeared on a live South Jersey radio show, *Carmen's Corner*. With its focus on local happenings, she'd had high hopes for attendance.

"Rumrunnerssssssss. I love that word," Carmen had said, drawing out the last letter until he ran out of breath. "And I do love rum."

He went on to describe all the drinks he'd had involving rum in any way until there was only one minute left in the segment for Nan's pitch.

"Please come to the Pinetree Town Library for an evening program on the rumrunners of South Jersey, featuring a local history expert, and we would especially love to hear stories from the audience about rumrunners in their families, and we will have lots of refreshments too." Nan rushed to the finish line.

On program night, three guys showed up. Nan didn't recognize any of them.

"Where's the bar?" one said, looking around the library meeting room.

"We heard on the radio there was free rum," another said.

She didn't want to tell them there was no bar, no rum, just a local history expert who had written an article on rumrunners in South Jersey during Prohibition, or she might lose her only audience.

"Stick around," she said, winking to imply that a rolling bar cart would be there any minute.

It worked. They sat down and stayed, although they constantly shifted in their seats and watched the door, waiting for the free booze. One of them did ask a question though. So he must have paid a little attention to the speaker.

After the program was over, Nan walked to a local bar on her way home and had three rums, one for each audience member, toasting the three men who had showed up.

Cheers to me. I'll take it. I'm calling that a small step in the right direction.

*

ON THE DAY of the glassblowing program, Nan was so nervous that she worried about vomiting while she introduced the speaker from the glass museum. She set a wastebasket by her side, just in case.

She made sure all the publicity described the program as a hands-on experience, not a lecture, hoping that would be immensely more appealing. The museum sent their mobile glassblowing studio with an actual little rolling furnace. They set up outside on the library's front lawn. A few people started to gather. Nan didn't know if they were there on purpose or if they had wandered by on their way to get their first ice cream of late spring; it was a beautiful Saturday afternoon. The speaker was a sturdy woman wearing denim overalls, reminding Nan of a Rosie the Riveter World War II-era factory worker, with her strong arms and back. Her booming voice commanded attention, all eyes on her from the minute she opened her mouth.

She started with a brief history of glassblowing right there in Pinetree, passing around gorgeous blue, red, and green flasks and bottles from the museum collection.

"I don't usually let people touch these," she said. "But I trust you all. These are artifacts of your history. Your family members may have made these. I know you will handle them as if they were precious, which they are."

Nan watched people passing the flasks and bottles as if they were tiny newborn babies. They let their children touch them too. She was bursting with pride and happiness. She had made this happen. She had started something really good.

Trixie came outside to watch.

Oh god, please don't pass the glass to Trixie. She's such a klutz. So far at work, Trixie had broken two lamps, a toilet, and had somehow shoved a printer off a table and smashed it.

"No, thank you," Trixie said when the bottles came her way, as if she was refusing a beverage she didn't want.

So she's not a total goofball. She knows her weaknesses.

The crowd grew as the demonstration went on. People

oohed and *ahhed* as the glassblower demonstrated her craft. She picked a teenager from the crowd to try her hand at a simple molten glass ball ornament. The kid grinned as though she'd won the lottery and performed enthusiastically. No one seemed to want to leave.

Finally, Nan led a round of applause for their speaker and invited the crowd to come back in two weeks for the last program in the series, the Jersey Devil program.

CHAPTER THIRTY-TWO

"WE SAW A terrible accident," Franny reported with great excitement after Nan opened her door and found her and Regina there. "A van crashed and rolled over right in the middle of the Atlantic City Expressway."

"And caught on fire," Regina added as if it was live entertainment for them, the fire a bonus like an encore at a concert.

They had popped up in Pinetree one Saturday afternoon. What an almighty shock. They'd never visited Nan when she lived in Philly. Because, of course, they were scared by what they saw on the nightly news: street corner shootings; mobs of kids rampaging down Market Street beating up passersby and grabbing things out of stores; even buildings in Philly attacked people, with old crumbling facades falling randomly on pedestrians. Nan was sure they thought that stuff went on every minute, that walking to the grocery store or riding the trolley was taking your life in your hands.

They hadn't asked Nan if they could visit. They'd left a message on her phone that they were "swinging by" that weekend. No one swung by Pinetree. It wasn't on the way to anywhere. Nan happened to have the weekend off—two whole days with nothing to do. She supposed she could show Franny and Regina around, maybe take them down to Atlantic City to gamble in one of the casinos or to the Pine Barrens for a hike. Did they gamble? Did they hike? She had no idea.

"Come in," Nan said.

If you must. Oh hell, they both have overnight bags in their hands. What have I done to deserve this?

She'd hardly gotten them inside when Immaculata came charging upstairs with a full tray of food and a jug of wine in a bag slung over her shoulder. Nan gave up. This whole thing was out of control.

"They don't drink," she told Immaculata, gesturing to Franny and Regina.

"We drink," they said, laughing.

Since when? Nobody tells me anything.

"You look like sisters," Immaculata said. "I would know you three were sisters anywhere."

"Do you have any sisters?" Franny asked, heaping cheese and crackers and olives on her plate. She took a big swig of wine.

"Too many," Immaculata said.

Franny and Regina laughed at everything she said as if she were a hilarious comedian. *Who are these cheery women? What have you done with my miserable sisters?*

Nan tried to be a convivial host. She shared stories of her favorite library users and the inside story of the delis in town and their specialties. She did her best Jersey Devil imitation, stomping around the room and flapping imaginary wings. She asked them how *they* were, and they started down their usual path, turning the conversation to their husbands, kids, and grandkids.

Every time she asked her sisters the simple question *How are you?* it was as if they did not exist apart from their husbands and children. *Are we still doing this, women of the twenty-first century?* Nan hoped to hear one of her sisters actually answer the question with *I'm bored* or *I'm thrilled* or *I'm horny* or *I'm anything* that was about their own personal individual life. *Who are you without others?* Nan longed to ask. *Who are you as a person? Who the hell are you?*

Then Franny rang her wineglass like a bell with her spoon as if she were making a toast at a wedding. "I have ants in my pants," she announced. "I want to go somewhere."

"Me too," Regina said. "We thought maybe you would come with us, Nan. A sisters' trip."

Kill me now.

"You don't travel," Nan said. *You two are afraid of every damn thing.*

"Things change," Regina said, throwing her hands up in the air.

"We could travel if you'd come with us," Franny said. "You know how; you've even been overseas."

To her sisters, a few short trips to Europe with an ex who'd paid for everything and never let Nan forget it made her an exotic adventurer, a modern-day Lady Hester Stanhope traversing the Syrian desert in the early 1800s.

"Think about it," Regina said. "We need to celebrate. We all made it past forty-seven. That's something to celebrate. We can relax now. We can enjoy ourselves."

Nan hated to admit it, but she knew exactly what Regina meant. Every woman whose mother dies young knows.

The year Nan had turned forty-seven, she'd been an absolute nervous wreck for the entire year, drinking far too much and too often to kill her terror. It was totally irrational, and she had even known it at the time. But she could practically hear the ticking bomb inside herself that had killed her mother at forty-seven. She felt as if she'd held her breath for the entire year, and then it took her the whole next year to believe she'd made it. She was still here; she could do what she wanted with her life.

"How many times have you thought you had cancer so far?" Nan asked her sisters.

"A million," Franny said.

"At least. More like a trillion," Regina said. "I'm sick of worrying about it. I'm done."

Nan looked at her sisters, seeing herself in a few years, their resemblance too close to deny. If she stopped getting edgy haircuts and dying her hair in crazy pastel streaks, if she gained a few pounds, if she stopped her vigilant opposition to looking, sounding, or acting like her sisters, the three of them could be triplets.

"What is wrong with us?" Nan said. "We spend our whole lives worrying about dying."

"Show her what you found." Regina urged Franny, who

pulled an old photo from her purse. She pointed to their mother in young womanhood and a striking young man who was not their father, with his cheek pressed to hers. Both were dressed in flashy red satin skating costumes. They were posed on a competition skating rink, in front of a scoreboard and judging stand. They looked like professional skaters. What on earth was this?

"Mom didn't skate," Nan protested.

"Oh, yes, she did," Franny said. "She was even a champion. They were pair skaters, together on the ice for years." She pointed to the man in the photo. "She was in love with him before Dad. And the guy died suddenly. He crashed his car into a tree. I found letters. Dad never even knew about him. He told me that Mom and he had only ever dated each other, that they only had eyes for each other."

This was what was wrong with their family. It was blindingly clear now. Nan visualized the incredible ripple effect of that huge raw wound of a secret—an unhappy marriage; a weepy wife stuck in unspoken grief who had settled for a life she didn't really want; a husband who eventually acknowledged that his wife would never be happy but stayed because he was a good guy, and good guys stayed until their lives went up in flames; and three daughters who grew up thinking this morass of sadness was how life had to be lived.

"I used to be so scared to come in the house after school that I peed my pants every day on the front step when I was in second grade," Nan said. "I was scared to see Mom crying."

Regina squeezed her hand, a silent *sorry*. Franny shook her head and looked at Nan with real sympathy.

"Here's to the good old days. Before therapy and antidepressants." Regina raised her glass in a toast, making them all laugh ruefully.

"To the bad old days, may they never return." Franny held her glass high.

For once, Immaculata was silent. Nan looked at the photo for a long time before she gave it back to Franny. They all paused to watch Franny tuck it away again.

A quiet understanding began to bloom in Nan's body. This moment was more holy to her than the day she stood over her mother's grave, knowing nothing about her really.

She wished her mother had been able to hit the bottom of her grief and then rise up to feel joy again, every day. She wished three new baby girls smiling up at her mother had been enough to heal her pain permanently. She wished her mother's whole life had not been sliding down into black holes and crawling back out of them again. She wished she could have one more time to sit on a couch with her sisters on one of their mom's good days as she read to them from their favorite *Grimm's Fairy Tales*, making a deep scary wolf's voice. Nan still loved the part when the mother cuts open the wolf's belly, frees her children inside, and then fills the wolf up with rocks so when he goes to drink from the river, he falls in and drowns. She and her sisters always cheered at that part.

Franny rooted around in her purse again and slid a handwritten list on the table. "So how's next May for our sisters' trip? Nan, you can even pick the place from this list we made up."

Nan summoned up her favorite Dorothy Parker quote, *What fresh hell is this?* It was a great list, though, full of places she'd love to go to: Lisbon, Madrid, Rome, Edinburgh.

"We spent a lot of time on this list," Franny said. "Research."

"You'd be crazy not to go." Immaculata bossed Nan in her usual way.

Like she was in charge of Nan's life, not Nan.

"Who asked you?" Nan responded automatically.

Franny and Regina looked shocked at her rudeness.

This is how we talk to each other. We say things straight out. Nan realized Immaculata had taught her that. Because in her own family, no one ever said what they really meant. To-day's revelations certainly made that clear.

"Go while you all can." Immaculata plowed ahead. "Be-cause you never know."

Franny and Regina nodded like they were listening to the wisdom of the ages.

"Hey, Mac. You come too," Franny urged Immaculata.

They've been here five minutes, and they're already call-ing her by a nickname I didn't know she had.

"I'm not allowed to leave the state," Immaculata refused, laughing.

Turning to Nan, Regina chanted, pounding on the table. "It's all on you, Nan. Let's go go go go go go go." Franny and Immaculata chimed in.

It's that damn homemade red wine. But Nan had drunk enough that she agreed to Lisbon the following spring, and the women all cheered.

"They have a castle in Lisbon from the sixth century, way up on top of a hill overlooking the city," Regina said. "We better get in shape; we're going to be walking up there and all over that city." She looked ten years younger at that moment, lit up with excitement and flushed with wine.

"Nan, did you know Lisbon has the oldest bookstore in

the entire world still operating?" Franny announced. "The. Oldest. In. The. Entire. World." She repeated it slowly as if Nan needed to hear it again, to comprehend the wonder of it.

What a can of worms I've opened here.

Nan pictured Franny and Regina in full planning mode, their emails streaming at her for months up ahead, with information on each and every attraction in Lisbon. She was as excited as they were. It might not be a real good idea to encourage them too much way ahead of time though.

She was afraid they'd had such a good time in Pinetree they would never leave, but finally, the next day they got ready to go.

"Take her with you. She's a pain in my ass." Nan pretended to drag Immaculata by the elbow toward the car.

They all laughed, Immaculata most of all. Nan was reminded of the merriment of the older women in Barbara Pym's novels, finding the absurd and pleasurable in everyday life. She never thought she'd be lucky enough to find a gang of women to laugh with like this. Amazing that her sisters were two of them. Stunning that the gang she was laughing with was in Pinetree, New Jersey, of all the unlikely places on earth.

She had not seen any of this coming; how could she? What else was up ahead was a complete mystery to her now.

*

NAN COULDN'T BELIEVE her eyes. Statues of saints rolling by on white pedestals right down the middle of Main Street after being hauled out of St. Anthony's Church. Crowds of spectators lining the street. The high school marching band playing what sounded like the hokeypokey; that couldn't be right.

"What's all this?" Nan asked a cop standing at an intersection near a barricade.

He snorted at her ignorance. "Only one of the oldest Italian festivals in the entire country. Started by immigrants back in the 1800s to ask Our Blessed Mother Mary for a good harvest and to thank her for their safe passage here. Where've you been?"

Come to think of it, she had seen posters everywhere and a giant banner across the street. But she thought an Italian festival was about meatball and sausage sandwiches, amateur bands singing Frank Sinatra songs, cheesy carnival rides, maybe cannoli stands. This parade of rolling saints was totally unexpected.

Nan decided to watch the saint parade for a while to see if she could figure out what this was all about. Were the saints leading the way to the meatball and sausage sandwiches?

It was quite hypnotic, the slow-moving crowd singing hymns, people pushing wheelchairs and baby carriages, marchers with kettle drums and trumpets keeping a ragged rhythm. When Our Lady of Guadalupe rolled by, the singing was in Spanish and was much livelier than the dirge-y hymns sung in English. First, Italian immigrants came to this town built on Lenni Lenape land, now Mexican immigrants. Who would be next? From what she could see, this was as much a march of history and cultures as it was a religious procession.

To her surprise, she spied Mona shuffling along in a crowd of other women behind a float arrayed with roses and decorated with a massive Rosary with beads the size of beach balls, topped by the biggest Mary statue she'd ever seen. Impulsively, Nan joined her, startling Mona.

"Where are you going with that giant Mary?" Nan really wanted to know.

"I can't talk. We pray while we walk," Mona said.

Now that everyone on the sidelines saw her there, Nan felt she had to keep going. Otherwise, it would feel like leaving a theater five minutes into act one. It was a lurching procession, some of the statues rolled along by altar boys and girls in their garb, others by priests and nuns, and more by members of the Knights of Columbus in their plumed hats. Everyone looked hot as hell, sweat dripping down faces and staining underarms.

When the procession was over, Mona quickly reverted to her usual loquacious know-it-all self to fill Nan in. "My mother couldn't get pregnant. Six years they were married, *nothing*. Finally, she walked this procession behind the Blessed Mother, praying all the way." Mona paused for dramatic effect, leaning close to Nan. "The very next year, she walked behind the Blessed Mother with *me* in a baby carriage. So there."

Was Mona hoping for a blessed event of her own? Was there a grandchild slow in arriving?

No, it seemed Mona was required to do it. She explained that her mother had walked the procession every year after for the rest of her life, had six more children before she died, and had pledged Mona would continue the tradition to give thanks.

Nan wondered how many of the women here were marching for fertility. It was probably no more farfetched than a lot of the other alleged infertility cures. There were a ton of books on the subject that people requested at the library—on Chinese herbs, acupuncture for fertility, how to cook with sea moss and wild yams, and her favorite, hypnosis.

Ding of a calming bell. Close your eyes and imagine a baby in your arms. Not a baby with a stinky diaper. No, not a baby puking over your shoulder. *Stop that, imagine a sweet-smelling baby.* Nan would not be good at being hypnotized; she could just tell. Her mind wandered too much.

Mona pulled an older woman over and urged her to tell Nan her story. The woman had a beaming face, a misshapen torso, and she held herself up with braces and canes.

"I almost died when I was born. My two grandmothers stood over me all night long praying to Mary to save me. They didn't have no doctors back then, no hospital. But they had this procession the next day. They had Mary to pray to for help. By the time the procession was over, I was out of trouble. And here I am today." She clearly had told the story many times, but she choked up with real emotion.

The meatball sandwiches that came later were phenomenal, but what Nan could not stop thinking about was the power of the stories the women had told. This town held a deep vein of lore that erupted at every opportunity; she felt wrapped in stories here.

CHAPTER THIRTY-THREE

THE NIGHT OF the Jersey Devil program, it poured so hard the streets started to fill up as the drains stopped working. The sound of rain pounding on the roof was all Nan could hear in the library, but she ignored it and continued to set up chairs in the meeting room, every single folding chair they owned.

The first heart-stopping moment was when the speaker, the author of a book on the Jersey Devil, turned up only five minutes before the program's start time, apologizing profusely for his lateness. He'd had to drive at a very slow pace on the expressway because of all the accidents.

Her second crushing fear, now that he had made it, was

that no one else would show up. The room was still full of empty chairs, and it was almost time to begin.

This was the worst part of giving library programs for adults. If it was just her, no problem. She could chalk it up to the weather and something good on TV and call it a night. But if a speaker drove there in terrible weather, the very least they should get for their trouble was a full house. The very worst-case scenario was when only one person came to a program. Then, she'd have to let the program proceed. If no one came, she could cancel it, give the author his check, and go home early to drink heavily.

When Chuck and Mr. El came in, shaking off rain like a pair of wet dogs, Nan wanted to hug them. When Lolly came in with her three oldest children, Nan made sure they got special Jersey Devil bookmarks. When a bus pulled up from the senior center and ten bedraggled elders spilled in, she collected all their wet coats and umbrellas and escorted them to front seats. When vans pulled up full of Boy Scouts and Girl Scouts, Nan felt like cheering. The door kept opening and opening, the meeting room was full, and now people were standing in the back of the room. But when Joe and Immaculata came in, Nan thought she might faint from shock.

"What are you looking at?" Immaculata asked. "I told

you I'd leave the house if there was something I wanted to see in this town. I never seen this before."

The only one missing was Jeremy. He had initiated the whole idea that night at dinner and had talked of nothing else for the whole month. Where was he? Maybe the crowd was so big, Nan just couldn't see him.

Nan and Dunkan raced to drag in chairs from other parts of the library. It was a miracle. She'd never seen the place this full. She was so nervous, hoping the author could project his voice loudly enough that everyone could hear. They didn't own a microphone, had never needed one before.

She thanked the crowd for coming, then introduced the speaker and the format of the program, with the author talk for the first part and the storytelling for the second part.

"Our speaker tonight is collecting more Jersey Devil stories, so your story might become part of his next book," she explained.

This was the biggest crowd she'd ever addressed in her whole career. Her voice sounded eerily like her annoying sisters, as if Regina and Franny were inside her head and she couldn't separate herself from them. She had the wholly disconcerting feeling that her mouth was opening and closing, but she had no idea what words she was actually saying.

Please let me make sense. Please let me sound smart, welcoming, friendly. Please let me pull this off.

The author, a fey young man from Philly, queer if Nan's gaydar was working, had spent many weekends camping out in the Pine Barrens hoping to have his own encounter with the Jersey Devil. The creature had been described by eyewitnesses since the 1800s as winged, hairy, much taller than a human, with a horselike head, goat haunches, and a tail. The author started with a history of sightings and the panics they'd caused over the decades, including a famous one all the way up in Philadelphia in 1909 that had the Philadelphia Zoo offering a $10,000 reward for the creature's capture.

"I never saw it myself," he confessed. "I want to, so badly. I did find evidence though."

He showed photos of footprint tracks that were like no other species ever found. He played a recording of an eerie inhuman scream he'd recorded deep inside the Pine Barrens forest. The pièce de resistance was a photograph of dead pigs, ripped apart in a frenzy of destruction, attributed to an extremely hungry Jersey Devil.

When the author invited the audience to share their encounters, there was a long silence that seemed to Nan to last a whole hour. She didn't know what to do. All these people were waiting, but no one was speaking up.

Finally, a young man dressed in a work uniform with an HVAC company logo stood up and cleared his throat nervously.

"Last year, I was driving my work truck, and I decided to take a shortcut home on one of the dirt roads through the Pine Barrens because it was so late, and I knew I could cut off a half hour or so. I was dying to get home. It had been a long day, full of problems and delays. I was so tired I could hardly see straight, but I hadn't been drinking, and I wasn't so sleepy I couldn't drive safe."

He spoke looking straight at the author. He was shy, Nan realized. He was afraid to look around him and see how many people were turned in their seats listening to him.

"My truck stalled out all of a sudden. I lost power; my headlights went out too. I got out, looked under the hood, trying to see what was wrong. But it was so dark—there's no lights out there. My flashlight could only do so much against that kind of darkness. So then..."

Nan felt the whole audience lean toward him.

"So then, my head still under the hood, I heard this sound over my shoulder, a sound like nothing I've ever heard before. It was a flapping, like the biggest bird you could ever imagine was over my head, coming at me. And I smelled the strangest smell, like nothing I've ever smelled before."

Joe and Nan looked at each other. His face lit up as if he was saying *See, I told you. I'm not crazy, I smelled the Jersey Devil too.*

The man hunched his shoulders and ducked his head to reenact the encounter. "I kept my head down like this. I was afraid the thing was coming at my head. *Flap flap flap*—it kind of hovered over me. It seemed like it lasted forever but probably a few minutes, and then it went away."

The man sat down quickly. No one asked him a question. No one waited to see if he wanted to add anything. But he had opened a floodgate. Three other people stood up, racing to tell the next story, then two more, then three more.

Nan's favorite was the farmer who started with a litany: "Now, I know foxes, I know bears, I know coyotes, I know bobcats. I know all the predators around here. I know raccoons that pull the legs right off rabbits in hutches. I know foxes that love a fat duck for dinner. But I do not know what this animal was that I passed on my farm road. I do not know an animal that stands that tall. I do not know an animal with haunches like a goat. I do not know a head like a horse and wings like a bat. That is what I saw that night. If it wasn't the

Jersey Devil, then I'll be damned."

The program went on and on. No one wanted to go home. Finally, Mona signaled to Nan that it was time to close, and Nan led the crowd in a round of applause for the author. There was no time for him to sign books, but he sold out that night, with people grabbing a copy on their way out and handing him money.

Joe drove Nan and Immaculata home. The truck smelled of a million oil changes and many rides given to Joe's farmer friends and their dogs. Nan leaned back, so exhausted she literally couldn't speak.

"You did good." Immaculata patted her hand.

Joe didn't say anything, but his head bobbed like he was saying *Yes Yes Yes* as he turned down the gravel driveway to home.

Before Nan fell asleep, she pictured Jeremy's face when he talked about the Jersey Devil, the way his eyes lit up with amazement at such a good story.

She hoped he was there. But if he was there, way in the back of the crowd, why didn't he stay behind and talk to her afterward? He should have been hanging out near the author or helping put chairs away. He should have been the last one to leave.

*

WHERE WAS JEREMY? As suddenly as he had appeared in the library every day when Nan was the new Town Librarian, he disappeared just as quickly. It had been four days since the Jersey Devil program that he missed, almost a week since he'd camped out in his favorite spot in the Reference Room, half hidden by the stack of books he always had arranged around him.

Nan grew more afraid with every day that went by. She stopped at the middle school office, but no one would tell her anything. He always came by himself to the library, so she didn't know his school friends to ask. Amo had been helping him look up colleges and scholarships, but he didn't know where Jeremy was either.

Finally, she drove out to the address he had listed on his library card application and asked to speak to the woman who had signed it. She didn't work there anymore, and everyone was gone, the man who answered the door said.

"Can you help me? I'm looking for Jeremy Murphy. I'm the town librarian. You can tell me. Is he okay?"

The man shook his head and shut the door.

In desperation, Nan went to see Pip. She explained how

close the boy had gotten to Immaculata and Joe, how unusual it was for him to disappear from the library with no notice, how she really needed to find out where he was and if he was okay.

Pip listened without saying a word. He pulled a file from a drawer and opened it. Then he picked up a pencil and laid it down on the paper pointing to a section. Finally, he put his finger to his lips and left the room.

So that she could read the paper. So that she could absorb the fact that Jeremy had been transferred to another school district, all the way up north to Newark. So that she could know the truth without Pip breaking confidentiality and probably a million other legal restrictions he'd just violated in order to help her out.

Her pain at the news was equal to her relief at knowing he was okay. Jeremy was gone. Now, all she had to do was break it to Joe and Immaculata.

*

THEY WERE QUIET when Nan explained. All three of them sat on the front porch in a sad little row. Immaculata nodded, sighed, and got up to put on hot water for tea. Joe didn't say a word as he rocked and rocked. Nan stayed with them for a while. Life felt like an unending series of losses sometimes. She tried to remember that meeting Jeremy was a gain; he wasn't dead, just moved away. Oh, what was the use. When you lost someone, no matter how, it hurt.

*

A WEEK LATER, Immaculata got a letter in the mail from an address in Newark, addressed to Nan, Joe, and Immaculata in small, precise, cursive handwriting. That kid—even his handwriting was on a college level. They sat down at the kitchen table, Immaculata reading the letter out loud.

> *Dear Immaculata and Joe and Nan,*
>
> *I am fine. How are you?*
>
> *I am very sorry I did not get to say goodbye to you. They came late at night and moved me. I didn't know they were going to.*
>
> *But Cleo (my new foster lady) helped me look up your address so I could write to you.*
>
> *Guess what? You won't believe it. Here I am in a big city, but I still have a garden. Hey, Joe, I am*

practicing everything you taught me. Me and Cleo belong to a community garden two blocks away. It's really cool, all lit up at night with fairy lights so we can grill and have picnics there. There's other kids my age that hang out there too. Our garden has tomatoes, peppers, and cucumbers (Did you know cucumbers can turn into pickles? We are growing a ton because Cleo loves pickles. She's teaching me how to cook them.) and a bunch of other stuff.

My new school is gigantic. We even have a school librarian. She saves books for me. Guess what, Nan, she's real, not a volunteer. She lets me read anything I want. On Saturdays, I get to go to the public library. You wouldn't believe how huge it is. It's the biggest library in the whole world, I think. Nan, you should come see it. I could give you a tour. I know the whole building already.

I miss making pizzelles with you, Immaculata. I miss everything (except that other place I was in, I'm glad they shut it down). But I am writing to

let you all know I am fine. It's just me and Cleo
here, and the house is very quiet, which I appre-
ciate. Cleo is cool. She reads practically as much
as me. Please write back. Please.

Your friend forever, Jeremy.

P.S. I love you too.

"Good." Joe touched the letter as if he were patting Jeremy's hair.

Immaculata cried. Joe held on to her, rubbing her back. She cried until she choked. She cried until the tears streamed down her face and ran all the way down to her chest. She cried so hard she gasped for breath.

"Why are you crying? It's all good news." The sight of the old woman in tears shocked Nan.

"The boy likes it up there, honey," Joe said.

"I'm not crying," Immaculata said.

"What do you call that water on your face?" Nan asked.

"I was cutting up onions."

Nan held out her arms to Immaculata, who swatted them away. That was more like it. That was more like the valiant Immaculata she knew and loved.

"You big old crybaby," Nan said.

"Get out of here before I stab you with a fork."

"Not if I get to you first."

Immaculata laughed, wide-mouthed, eyebrows raised, pretending to be shocked. "You're getting the hang of it."

The hang of what? How to live with loss? How to make a joke out of pain? How to laugh at sadness and start over? How to manage the mixture of grief and joy that was life? Whatever Immaculata meant, Nan was absurdly happy at the compliment.

*

"CAN YOU PICTURE Jeremy's face when he gets this?" Nan took one last look inside the care package they had put together for him.

She'd wrapped up the Jersey Devil book from the library program he had missed. Immaculata packed a huge batch of pizzelles and his other favorite, thumbprint cookies, with her homemade blueberry jam in the middle. Joe went to Chuck's hardware store and bought a small toolbox, then packed it full of shiny new tools: a hammer, all kinds of screwdrivers, pliers, and wrenches, and a retractable measuring tape in a solid silver shell that made a satisfying zip when it rewound itself.

They included a thank you card to Cleo. How inadequate, Nan felt, but it was the best way they could express their mass of emotions that Jeremy was safe and happy with her. Especially because Cleo had cared enough to keep Jeremy in contact with people who loved him. He had lost enough in his short life; Cleo must have recognized that and actually done something about it.

To Jeremy, they each wrote separate letters so he'd have a lot to open up. It figured, Immaculata's letter was three pages long, flowing out of her with the same velocity as her words did. She wrote about the tracks she'd found in the backyard, which she was certain were a bobcat's, even though they were so rare in South Jersey. She recounted a new Jersey Devil sighting, very coincidentally on the very same night as the library program, and how she was suspicious of the timing and the motives of the storyteller (who was known to be a jokester). But she wrote down every detail to tell him anyway, just in case.

Nan sent a photo of Immaculata and Joe laughing, standing in front of their sunflowers, along with a list of books and authors Jeremy might like. He always wanted reading suggestions. Charles Dickens and Jules Verne would keep him busy for quite a while. But she put five stars next to *The Diary of a*

Young Girl by Anne Frank, hoping he would start there, now that he knew there was no such thing as a boy book or a girl book.

Joe wasn't much of a writer, but he made a little drawing of each tool and noted what to use each one for. "Oh boy. He's going to be so happy." His eyes were lit up with a joy that radiated so strongly Nan pictured it reaching all the way to Jeremy's new home.

CHAPTER THIRTY-FOUR

IMMACULATA BANGED ON the inner door.

Nan sighed. That woman had the worst timing sometimes. But Nan put on a T-shirt and opened the door a tiny
crack. "Who is it?" she trilled as if it could be anyone else but
Immaculata.

"Joe didn't come home." Immaculata shoved the door
open and burst in. Her hair stood up in gray tufts, her
housedress rumpled.

Nan had been lingering in bed. She'd woken up before
dawn, dying to finish her mystery book about a village librarian in the Cotswolds. Only two short chapters from the end,

both of the protagonists were in dire straits, and she had absolutely no idea who had murdered the beloved village librarian.

Nan had never seen Immaculata so distressed. She gave off panic waves, her eyes wild with fear.

"He went out last night with the dogs like he does, but he always comes home by now," she said. "He never showed up at Stumpy's for breakfast with the guys either. We need to go look for him. Right now."

Nan drove Joe's truck over to the lake, Immaculata gripping the door handle hard. It was still very early; no other cars were in the lake's parking lot; no runners or walkers were on the path around the lake; no children played on the playground swings.

They heard it before they saw it—a chorus of dogs barking insistently, louder and louder as they approached. Joe lay curled beneath a huge pine tree, the dogs surrounding him in a protective circle. They quieted down as Immaculata called Joe's name, laid her cheek on his, tried to rouse him, and finally wailed to Nan to call an ambulance.

The EMTs were so kind. They told Immaculata to take all the time she needed. The chief knew Joe, as so many people in town did. He held Immaculata's hand, sitting next to

Joe's body. Joe's heart had stopped, and it was a quick and painless way to go, he reassured her. Remember that time Joe climbed up on the water tower to erase graffiti, and he fell coming down and broke his leg, how he kept pleading to the EMTs "Don't take me to the emergency room." He was terrified of it; people died in there. That time, we had to take him. But this way was better, right? He died by the lake; he loved this lake. He died with his friends around him, these dogs. Hey, wasn't that the mayor's dog?

He kept talking, patting her hand, painting a picture of Joe going to sleep here by the lake. Until Immaculata could get up on her feet. Until Joe's body was loaded onto the stretcher. Until she climbed in with him.

*

"NO FUNERAL," IMMACULATA said. Joe's friends stood in the doorway.

"Immaculata, please let us in." Stumpy Locatore gestured to the guys lined up on the driveway, the farmer gang from the red barn café.

"And no Catholic nothing. Joe forbid it. Ever since he found out about all those little kids the priests abused, with the popes, cardinals, bishops, all of them covering it up for so many years all over the world. He almost lost his mind altogether about it. Joe would not rest if I put him anywhere near Catholic anything."

"Okay, okay," Stumpy said, raising his hands in surrender.

"I mean it. No funeral. You're not going to talk me out of it," she said. "You might as well go home." But clearly, she had no real fight in her. She turned and walked back to the kitchen, leaving the front door open.

The guys wiped their feet, one by one, and entered. They leaned against the counters, they filled every seat, they stood in the doorway. Their eyes were downcast, they looked as shaken as Immaculata.

Nan filled up the big coffee urn and handed out mugs. The men passed the mugs along in an absurd assembly line, snaking back to her until she held one in each hand and looked down at them. How had that happened? She had no recollection of even making the coffee, but she must have. That same fog of disbelief she'd felt at the death of her parents had descended again, blurring memory and movement.

Immaculata laid her head down on the table. Stumpy put his hand on her shoulder. The breathing of the men seemed to fill up the air in the kitchen as if they were all breathing in unison.

"Okay," she said finally, lifting her head. "Let's get this show on the road. I need to bury Joe somehow. Call Sardone's."

The guys helped Immaculata write an obituary. They all struggled with that until Nan found a box of photographs. The men pawed through them, recognizing friends and relatives, telling stories about them and laughing. When they held up a photo of Joe with a huge smile on his face, surrounded by his dog pack, they all agreed that was the one.

*

THE DAY OF the funeral was sunny and warm. The funeral home sent the hearse to pick up Immaculata. Nan rode with her, as Immaculata had asked. That was a first for Nan. It felt oddly like what she'd imagined riding in a limousine en route to a happy occasion would feel like, all dressed up, watching the world from behind the glass, and being driven by a man in a fancy suit. There was no champagne in the hearse though.

Immaculata rode with her hand resting on Joe's coffin. Nan wondered why the funeral home hadn't left the coffin there, where the service was going to be held. But she hadn't been to a funeral since her father's when she was fifteen, the year after her mother's. That day, the day she called herself an orphan for the first time, was a big blank in her memory, with only snatches of images remaining of the nuns from school in black flapping habits like crows of death gathered around the hole in the earth. She shuddered at the memory.

The hearse drove slowly by the building where Sammy's tailor shop had been, continued down Main Street where scattered people stood on the curb, their heads bowed, Catholics making the sign of the cross as the hearse passed, then all the way out to the lake, where it drove through the parking lot and turned around.

"Where are we going?" Nan was confused by what seemed like an aimless drive around town.

"It's tradition," Immaculata said. "Don't they do this in the city? One last time for Joe to go by all the places he loved."

The hearse continued, past Stumpy's red barn café on a rutted farm road, where it bounced up and down slowly, and finally past Joe and Immaculata's house again.

"You didn't sign up for this, did you?" Immaculata turned to Nan with a tiny grin. "You thought you were going right to the funeral home, didn't you?"

A joy ride with a beloved dead person—this town is a whole new experience.

"Come to think of it, I didn't sign up for anything I got in this town," Nan said.

When the hearse pulled up in front of the funeral parlor, Immaculata didn't move. It seemed as if her legs wouldn't work. She stared out behind the curtained windows at the undertakers in their black suits, lined up beside the door.

"Too soon," she said. "Leave me alone."

Nan didn't argue with her. She asked the funeral ushers to wait. They all stood still, hands crossed in front of their bodies, for what seemed like a very long time. An organ played softly inside, notes escaping outside and flying up into the air around them.

"Joe's not really gone," Immaculata finally said. "He's on one of his long walks. He's out there all the time now." She sounded like she was talking to herself; Nan knew not to respond.

When she finally opened the door, Immaculata seemed to struggle to breathe, as if a great weight was crushing her chest. She leaned on Nan's arm and walked stiffly forward, following the coffin into the funeral parlor, where she sat down beside it. She didn't stand up to talk to the people who came to say goodbye to Joe, but they all leaned down to hug her or shake her hand.

*

AFTER THE SERVICE, the funeral director approached Nan while she was waiting for Immaculata to detach from the crowd. Nan noticed the director had the most lustrous long hair, like a beautiful pony. Long legs, too, encased in the requisite black pantsuit. But her eyes were what captured Nan immediately. She looked smart and deep, the kind of woman she could fall into conversation with and hours would go by like minutes.

She introduced herself as Sophia Sardone. Nan repeated it to herself automatically. What an enchantingly lovely name. Her voice reminded Nan of limoncello liqueur: tart-sweet, goes down easy, hard to stop once you start.

Nan berated herself. *Really, is a funeral of a man you loved the appropriate place to notice women? Get a grip.*

CHAPTER THIRTY-FIVE

THERE IT WAS, shimmering before her. Her absolute dream job—director of the Provincetown Public Library, the queerest town in America, on the tip of Cape Cod in Massachusetts. Home to artists, writers, and outlandish people, it had a fascinating history as a fishing village of Portuguese immigrants. Yes, Nan was still an occasional voyeur of job postings; it was an irresistible peek into other possible lives. She hadn't applied for a new job or even seriously considered another, though, since she'd been in Pinetree. But this was P'town—it was a paradise; it was a pleasure dome; it was a party.

What if Pinetree was just my warm-up act for P'town?

After all, Nan knew she had to work for a big new life. It wasn't just going to form automatically around her. She would do anything to get to P'town.

One of her exes had been enamored with P'town and brought Nan there for the first time; she only dated women who loved the place as much as she did. Nan had passed that test but had failed many others before that relationship crashed and burned.

After the relationship that brought her to P'town had painfully ended, Nan had returned there on her own or with other lovers. She had her first lobster there and could still taste the revelation of it. Her first bottle of excellent red wine. Her first Portuguese egg tarts and hand pies. Her first whole artichoke—which she had no idea how to eat until a kind server coached her to pull off a petal, dip it in butter, and suck it, pulling its lovely flavor through her teeth.

She walked everywhere there, enthralled by the mix of ancient tiny cottages and majestic captain's houses. She could sit for hours watching waves at the beach under skies so wildly blue and clouds so dramatically billowing that she understood how painters spent lifetimes trying to capture them. One winter holiday week, she'd even stayed in Provincetown all by herself. It had been incredibly blustery and cold, and she'd fallen even more in love with it.

Now she read the job description eagerly. Miracle of miracles, she actually had verifiable experience in everything they were looking for: management, budgeting, collection development, community relations, grant writing, programming for all ages, local history.

Is that really me? I look so good on paper now. And I'm as queer as can be. Hope I get extra points for that. She remembered applying for the Pinetree job, where she had bluffed and begged her way in.

She forced herself to take her time with the application, revamped her resume a million times, wrote ten different cover letters, and spent hours reading newspaper articles about what had been going on in the library and town recently. She even memorized the history of the library and read books written by famous residents and visitors—Mary Oliver, Jack Kerouac, Kurt Vonnegut. She drew the line at the detested Norman Mailer though.

Her heart pounded as she applied, wanting this so much that it hurt. For good luck, she wore her favorite faded Provincetown T-shirt. To ward off the jinx, she told no one. It was exactly what she needed after the sadness of losing Jeremy and Joe, a shining dream up ahead to look forward to.

CHAPTER THIRTY-SIX

LIFE WITHOUT JOE didn't make sense. How could everything just keep going: the phone ringing, the radio bringing news, Nan going off to work, the mail carrier bringing cards and letters to Immaculata from so many people who knew Joe. Nan guessed the wheels of the world never stopped.

Immaculata's sisters started to visit, especially Annunciata, who looked like Immaculata's twin without the birthmark. Nan loved when she came over. Annunciata was the perfect foil for her sister, and she never shut up, ending the awful silence in the house. Nan hung around when she was there.

While Annunciata was listing, in great detail, all the items on sale at the grocers that week, Immaculata interrupted, "My underpants fell down today, right in the middle of the garden."

Annunciata laughed so hard she almost fell off the porch bench but demanded to know how that happened.

"I'm getting skinny," Immaculata confessed. "I can't eat. They're so big on me now."

"That won't last," Annunciata said, patting her arm. "Just get new underwear in the meantime, before you give me a stroke from laughing so hard."

Later Nan asked Immaculata why she'd stopped talking to Annunciata and her other sisters so many years before. She shrugged, then slowly recounted the story of how she'd wanted to go to college so badly but her family laughed at her, told her girls don't go to college.

"All your sisters came to Joe's funeral. They sat right up front, remember?" Nan asked. She hoped a new memory would chase away the past.

"I don't remember a damn thing about that day," Immaculata said.

But Nan could see how much she counted on her sisters now, how time and grief had healed that old hurt.

*

NAN MISSED JOE every time she walked down Main Street and saw a dog in a yard looking hopefully at passersby. She missed hearing the steady clink of his shovel turning over dirt in his garden and the hissing of the hose when he watered. She missed seeing his eyes light up at something funny Immaculata said at dinner and watching his shoulders jiggle, laughing silently with her. She even missed the sight of his flannel shirts flapping on the clothesline.

If she got the job in Provincetown, she'd be leaving Immaculata in an empty house. That would be hard. But it was hard anyway. She had to follow this dream to the tip of Cape Cod. That was her special place, her landing place, the place that had been beckoning her all these years; she was sure.

*

NAN SPOTTED CHUCK in front of the hardware store. He hugged her like the close friend that he now was, delight lighting up his face and eyes. A young woman stood next to him, her arms full of plants.

"My daughter, Kennedy." He presented her with a flourish. "She's helping me out at the store."

Nan was so fiercely glad to see her out of rehab again,

back home with her family, and looking so fresh-faced and clear-eyed through the new tattoos that covered her neck and forehead that she hugged both Kennedy and her armload of purple and pink pansies. The flowers almost didn't make it, the potting soil in their container spilling out on both of them.

"I'm so sorry," Nan apologized. "I didn't mean to hug you. I should have asked. I am just so glad to meet you."

"Call her off, Dad," Kennedy said, laughing.

Nan brushed herself off, waved goodbye, and walked away. She then turned back to the beautiful sight of the father and daughter side-by-side, surrounded by flowers.

In Provincetown, there were so many gorgeous gardens. She had walked down every East and West End street there so many times that she could summon up the weathered fences with riotous pink rose bushes spilling over them, tall purple alliums poking up, cheerful black-eyed Susans, swaying tall grasses, and banks of violet hollyhocks.

She pictured herself in Provincetown, imagined a team of interviewers picking up her resume and waving it excitedly at one another—the perfect candidate for the library job, here she is. Let's meet *her* immediately.

Nan would have to find a stupendously perfect outfit for the interview that was sure to materialize. Nothing she had was special enough. Provincetown required funky panache, cool queer fashion. Was she up to it? Hell yes, she couldn't wait to get there. She was going to ace that interview.

*

"WHAT ARE YOU doing up there?" Immaculata shouted up. "You sound like a herd of elephants."

It was the day of reckoning, when Provincetown Public Library would notify applicants who were selected for an interview. Nan had taken the day off work so she would know instantly when her summons came. She started out the day walking in circles around her apartment, her nervous energy at an all-time high.

"None of your business," Nan shouted back. "Leave me alone, old lady."

For once, Immaculata listened and didn't bother her again.

By noon, Nan was glued to the computer screen, hitting refresh constantly. In case they called, she held her phone in her hand, checking to make sure the volume was on high and the reception was strong.

At 5:00 p.m. she checked to make sure that Cape Cod was on Eastern Standard Time. Maybe it was earlier there.

Maybe she still had an hour of hope left. But no.

Finally, she gave up. The business day was over. It was possible, though, that they were running a day behind in notifications. She was sure it was an incredibly popular position. They had probably received thousands of applications. She told herself there was still hope, that anything could have delayed the process. She went to bed with a bottle of wine, but she never slept.

For the next three days, she called in sick and repeated the entire previous cycle of hope, waning hope, and despair. Then she gave up and crawled into bed, knowing her dream was over.

*

AFTERWARD, PINETREE LOOKED so tiny and dull to her. She'd walked down every street so many times, been inside every store enough that she knew which shelves held which items. She was sick of seeing the same parade of faces around her every single day. The library regulars. The shopkeepers. The crossing guards. The dog walkers. The mail carriers.

She still had fifteen years to work, at least, before she could retire. Was this town her final destination in life? Was running this tiny library the best she could do?

In a fury, she rearranged entire sections of the library. The only remedy for her disappointment was to change something, anything. Let the new book aficionados hunt for where she moved them to. Let the newspaper readers go to the back of the building instead of dominating all the chairs in front. Let the preschoolers twirl around the Children's Room searching for the picture books, now replaced by encyclopedias. Reshelve the entire Reference Room in reverse order for absolutely no reason. Mona finally stopped her from dragging the entire children's section up to the first floor with a flat No.

Okay, she couldn't change a lot of things, but she could certainly change her hair. She stomped down the street to the hair salon in search of purple and green highlights to replace the turquoise and pink ones.

When she opened the door, she couldn't believe what she was seeing. *I must be in the wrong place. This shop is chock full of nuns. That can't be right. Maybe I've walked into a nun boutique. Is there such a thing?* She went back out again to check the shop sign.

It was the hair salon, and yes, it was overflowing with nuns. Round wrinkled nuns in black short habits reading *People, Glamour,* and *Bride* magazines and a curious style book of updos, *Buns, Buns, and More Buns.*

Nuns in Buns sounds like a really bad movie, one I'd watch after one too many cocktails on a rainy night. Nan could practically picture the movie poster.

Craggy-necked nuns bent back over the sinks with their sparse white hair covered with shampoo tufts. A fresh-faced baby nun sat on the floor, cross-legged and playing a game on her phone. More nuns at the styling stations held up hand mirrors to see the back of their new dos.

"You caught us at a busy time, love," the shop owner called out. She was red-faced and sweaty, as if juggling so many nuns was as hard as running a marathon. "It's the convent's quarterly visit."

Nan backed out slowly. Change was not easy. That was becoming increasingly clear. At least for her. Other people seemed to effortlessly get new jobs, move to new places, find new partners, sail through challenges, move through metamorphoses. She was thwarted at every turn, big and small.

CHAPTER THIRTY-SEVEN

NAN WAS QUIET for most of their secret book club meeting. She listened while the others enthused about what they were reading.

"I can read again." Chuck's exuberance lit up his face. "Have you any idea of the relief of that? I thought I'd go mad." His daughter Kennedy was still at home and stable in her recovery. "Guess what? I have discovered an entire realm of writing I never even knew existed."

"Graphic novels," Mr. El guessed.

"Victorian erotica," Lolly offered.

They all laughed and looked expectantly at Nan.

"Drawing a blank," she said.

"Humorists. Comedians. Funny writers." Chuck opened his arms with a voila gesture. "I am laughing myself silly every single night. Dorothy Parker, Fran Lebowitz, David Sedaris, Caitlin Moran, James Thurber, Mindy Kaling, Mark Twain, Tina Fey, P.G. Wodehouse, Wanda Sykes, Steve Martin. What a glorious jumble of voices."

"Oh, yeah, life is hilarious. Let's all have a chuckle to chase away despair," Nan blurted out. Way to derail a conversation. They all stopped and looked at her with concern.

Lolly touched her arm. "What despair?"

Nan spilled it all out—her dream job, her love of Provincetown, the humiliation of not even getting to the first round of interviews, and most of all, her shame. She felt shame weighing on her body as heavy as chainmail armor.

"Why is it that you feel shame, Nan?" Mr. El's face was soft, his caring evident.

"I don't know. I always feel ashamed about wanting. And I wanted this so badly."

"In philosophy, there are many theories about this subject. Is desire intrinsically destructive or is it a natural means to achieve harmony?" Chuck looked thoughtful.

"What exactly do you want, Nan? Is this only about the

job?" Lolly asked.

The minute Nan heard that, she knew that it wasn't. It was amazing to her, the power of airing thoughts out loud, of talking to friends about her feelings. She felt a shift inside her, a clarity starting to emerge.

"I want to keep growing. I don't want to be done, stuck in a slot for life. I'm not over, I'm just getting started," she almost shouted. She felt like pounding her fist on the table for emphasis, but she didn't need to; they got it.

A beautiful chorus came back to her from her friends, exactly the wave of caring and reassurance a person wanted to hear at a time like this. It was wonderful and appreciated, but Nan knew it ultimately didn't matter what they said. She had to figure this out for herself.

She felt a firm nub of definite belief bump up to the surface. Of course she wasn't done with newness. Of course she would keep growing. Of course there were surprises up ahead.

*

MINUTES LATER, CHUCK was hopping up and down impatiently outside the diner as Nan came out. What on earth was wrong with him?

"Can you come with me right now? Please?" he asked. His face was rearranging itself, eyes widening, mouth open, forehead moving as his eyebrows wrinkled this way and that.

Nan agreed to go with him. He looked possessed, maybe she could help with whatever he was going through. He drove hurriedly back to town and parked on Main Street in front of an empty storefront.

"When you said you wanted to keep growing, that you weren't done, I knew right away what I had to do," he said.

Now he unlocked the door to the empty storefront where the shoe repair shop had been. Why in the world had he brought Nan here? He refused to tell her, only that he had something to show her.

The shop still smelled of old shoes, even though it was empty. It was surprisingly spacious inside, with large front windows filling the space with sun. Even though Nan had never had a shoe repaired in her entire life, she was sad the store was gone. An empty storefront was like a missing tooth in the front of a mouth.

"We gave up trying to find a new shoe repair person and lure them to town. Apparently, it's a trade that's reviving but mostly in cities. There's not enough business in small towns," Chuck explained.

"We? Are you in the Chamber of Commerce too? The library board isn't enough for you?"

He looked embarrassed. "I own this building. Well, me and my wife."

"Wow, and the hardware store too? You're a regular tycoon."

He cleared his throat. "It's worse than that. I own a bunch of buildings on Main Street."

He must be rich. Nan was astonished at the thought. Chuck's hardware store was stuck back in the 1940s, with its ancient rickety shelves and wooden floors so worn with decades of foot traffic you could feel the ghosts of past townspeople beneath your feet. Chuck was famous for wearing the most raggedy T-shirts beneath worn flannel shirts. Honestly, he looked like he didn't have two nickels to rub together. He lived on Oak Street in a shabby Cape Cod house that could use a fresh coat of paint and new shutters, where Nan had often seen wash drying on a line in the tiny back yard. Even his bicycle was a piece of crap. It was easy to hear him coming with those screechy brakes and that rattling chain.

"Not just buildings," Chuck continued. "I am one of those..."

"Spit it out, man."

"Closeted multi-millionaires." He looked like he was in pain. "Hardly anyone knows. I actually despise money, and we give a lot of it away. My wife hates it too. But when it comes to this town, if I see something that money can help, that's when I get excited."

Immaculata had insisted this town had a lot of money flying around in it, but Nan hadn't really believed her.

"Wait. Help me understand this. You're rich."

"Pretty rich," he admitted. "Family money. Over the years, my family bought land wherever they could. We've been around here since the town was incorporated. It compounds, I guess."

Money goes where money is; that's what Immaculata says. Like a giant magnet, whap. I wouldn't know personally about that as I've never had a detectable amount to attract more.

Nan didn't like rich people, as a rule. The few she knew lived in a different world than she did, a world where the rules didn't apply to them, where they got whatever they wanted when they wanted it, and to top it off, they seemed to think others were always trying to take their money away from them. Icky.

As if he knew what she was thinking, trying to absorb this

new information about her friend, Chuck said, "I know. I don't like rich people either." They chuckled together, bringing them back to their usual warm selves.

"I brought you here because I have the most amazing idea." Chuck put his hands together as if he were praying.

"No, I will not train as a shoe repair person. I was born with no manual dexterity whatsoever." Nan mimed tapping on a shoe sole with a shoemaker's hammer.

No dexterity except for the amorous arts, of course.

"Close your eyes."

She could see that he was deadly serious; she did it even though it felt ridiculous.

"What's the one thing this town—and all of South Jersey—really needs and doesn't have?"

Pinball arcade? Korean barbecue? Vegan convenience store?

"Picture this whole room filled with brand-new books. Picture beautiful editions of nursery rhymes and fairy tales that people will buy as gifts for families with new babies. Picture irresistible cookbooks with full-color photos. Picture being surrounded by piles of shiny bestsellers, snatching up the brand-new book by that author you love the minute it comes out. Picture a packed murder mystery aisle to die for. Picture a classics corner, fat with the wisdom of the ages. Now open your eyes and tell me if you can see it—the new, first-ever, Pinetree Bookstore."

Nan looked around the bare room and allowed herself the pleasure of the images. There was nothing more intoxicating than new books.

"Don't forget local history and cultures," she said. "Lenni Lenape, the indigenous people. South Jersey's Pine Barrens. Blueberry and cranberry preserving. Guides to iron furnaces of the Revolutionary War and abandoned villages. Hiking and kayaking guides. Glass antique collector's guides and histories of the glassblowing industry. All the Jersey Devil books and a life-size Jersey Devil sculpture right over there. People would go nuts over that."

Chuck reached out and held her hand with both of his. "I want you to manage it, Nan."

Me? Manage a bookstore? She felt exactly like Mildred Lathbury in Barbara Pym's *Excellent Women*, who compared love to a white rabbit thrust suddenly into your arms, a charming notion, but what do you do with it?

She was a librarian to her core. Books should be free for the using. Books shouldn't be only for people with the money to buy them. In the library, she could press books on everyone. Here, she'd watch people longingly pick up books, turn over to see the price, and put them down again. She had been that kind of person her whole life. Books were so expensive.

"Not just manage it," he added. "Be my partner."

"I don't understand."

"This is my big dream. I can't do it without your expertise. I want to make it worth your while."

"Chuck, if it's your big dream, why don't you run it?"

He sighed, searching for words. "I can't explain it really. I just know I don't want to be in a bookstore all day long. Hardware, though, that soothes me, makes me happy."

Nan waited. This still didn't make sense to her.

"I am overstimulated by books," he finally admitted. "I can't live surrounded by them. I would lose my grounding, go someplace else in my head where I wouldn't be able to take care of my family and myself. Does that make any sense?"

"Too much of a good thing?" Nan was reminded of the pleasures of alcohol, sipping until that magic point of just right.

"Yes, yes, yes, that's exactly it."

Where does that leave me? I'm still standing here feeling like I'm holding that wriggling white rabbit and don't know what to do with it.

"My head is spinning. I can't grasp all this," she said.

"The accountant will explain it all to you. I can't. All I want to do is beg you to consider this, after you hear the details. Will you, my friend?"

Of course she would consider it. She loved this man. It was a stunning idea. She didn't know if she could make what felt to her like an immense journey from librarian to bookseller. She even hated the word *bookseller.* It sounded like baby buying. Babies should not be for sale to the highest bidder and forbidden to poor people. The same for books.

But she asked for the keys so she could come back on her own. She wanted to sit quietly in the space on her own. She admitted to herself that those ideas for the bookstore had flowed out of her awfully easily just then. This whole caper felt like pure fun.

Was this the sound of a door opening in her life? Not the door she'd hoped for, but a door nonetheless.

CHAPTER THIRTY-EIGHT

A JOLLY ACCOUNTANT. What were the odds? The man chuckled and guffawed all the way through his unintelligible explanation of the contract he was presenting to Nan.

She had heard a big number. That was about as much as her brain could process.

"What's this again?" She pointed to the number.

"Your salary as the bookstore manager."

That can't be right. It's four times the salary I'm making now. I could help Jeremy pay for college. I could take so many trips. I could actually save money so that my eighty-year-old future self won't go hungry or without heat.

He explained that Chuck wanted to put her in the strong-est possible financial position. So he would remain the bookstore owner indefinitely and keep all the risks of running an independent small bookstore, but Nan would own the en-tire building outright. The building was the valuable asset. The big salary was to ensure the taxes and upkeep were not a bur-den. The apartment on the second floor was all hers too. She could live in it rent free or rent it out. If she rented the apart-ment out, she kept the proceeds. Store profits would also be hers, of course. Chuck would pay for all the necessary reno-vations and would lease the store *from her* at fair market prices, so she'd always have an income stream no matter how the store did.

"Why would he do that? Lease his own building back. It's his building." She would never understand high finance.

"He's a very generous man. He has a lot of money to give. He does this kind of stuff all the time. I'm not allowed to divulge specifics, but I can tell you he's propped up many of the small businesses around here, no strings attached. I'm the luckiest accountant alive to work with him." He chortled at Nan.

She was completely overwhelmed. It was all too much to absorb. She had lived paycheck to paycheck for thirty years.

Any little luxury she had, like a few days in Provincetown, went on a credit card that she struggled to pay off for the rest of the year. Now Chuck wanted to give her a building, a huge salary, profits from a business, and a rent-free apartment. It sounded stone-cold crazy to her.

"No pressure of course," Chuck said afterward. "I know it's a big decision. So you can let me know by tomorrow." He chuckled at the shock on her face.

"Really, when?"

"Take all the time you need." He patted her hand. "Day after tomorrow would be fine."

"You think you're funny?"

Then calm and philosophical Chuck, her steadiest, sweetest friend, leapt up and danced what she could only call jetés and pirouettes around the old shop, pointing to the corners, and naming them as he twirled by: classics corner, local history there, bestsellers right up front, philosophy there, cookbooks corner, children's corner there.

"There are only four corners, man. You just named six." She poked him as he swooshed by.

The joy on his face. He had been through so much pain with his daughter's addiction; he deserved to enjoy every exuberant move, every shining, hopeful vision.

*

NAN DIDN'T TELL Immaculata any of this. She wasn't in the mood to hear more opinions, and that woman was full of them. She was also full of surprises.

"I'm kicking you out," Immaculata announced.

"What in the world are you talking about?" Nan had to reel herself back in from the painful place she'd been in her head, the place where she worried about her choice, feared both making the biggest mistake of her life and missing the biggest opportunity of her life.

She felt like a woman in a horror movie with viewers screaming *Don't go through that door* at her, but which door was the door to keep shut and which one was the one to fling open?

"Annunciata needs to move in with me. She don't want to live with her kids; they drive her crazy. So I'm kicking you out so she can have your apartment. It's better for you anyway. You don't want to hang around with old ladies. You're young."

"How soon?" Nan had no lease, no leg to stand on.

"Not right away. She has to sell her house and get rid of a bunch of stuff."

The universe was trying to tell Nan something. But what?

"Don't worry. You can come over to dinner every night if you want," Immaculata said.

Like that's all I'm worried about.

Well. I will miss that.

*

AFTER MAIN STREET closed down for the night, the old shoe repair shop was a haunted place. Nan didn't want anyone passing by to see her there, so she sat on the floor with her flashlight and hoped no mice would run over her lap.

She let herself breathe the place in. The floors creaked and popped. The faint animal smell of old leather lingered. The cast iron radiators gurgled like a stomach full of good food.

How would they get enough bookshelves in here, with all those radiators taking up half the wall space? If she were in charge, she wouldn't allow them to be removed to make more room, absolutely not. They were beautiful useful objects, pleasingly curved warmth-givers. She believed in old things that still worked great.

Wait, was that herself she was talking about or the radiators?

No games, she decided. No toys. No crafts. No library-scented candles. No socks with quotations on them. No T-shirts. Definitely no story time corner. The bookstore was not going to compete with the library story time right down the street. No coffee. There was a wonderful coffee shop right across the street. She wasn't going to put them out of business.

Yes to a custom Pinetree Bookstore mug though. She loved bookstore mugs, especially the ones in classic diner shapes. And matching bookmarks—that would be appropriate.

But if she ran the bookstore, visitors would smell books. They would be surrounded by books, and they would absolutely know they were in an actual store full of books and mainly books, without a doubt. A kind of book heaven.

This was still really Chuck's dream though. Living in the library world had been the closest thing to a dream she'd had. But she'd been in that world so long it now felt like a recurring dream, the kind that when she woke up, she'd say, "I had that dream again," and it was always the same, with small variations.

Nan often dreamed of having to take care of babies, startling dreams where no one else was feeding the baby and she had to, no one else was saving the baby from the speeding car and she had to, no one else was rescuing the baby from the raging fire so she had to. According to the dream theory books she pored over, looking for answers, she was actually the baby, saving herself over and over again. She was the helpless and the helper, the adult and the baby, all in one. She hated that recurring dream; it was exhausting to be all things to herself.

She shone the flashlight slowly around the store one last time, turning it into a searchlight. She was searching for a sign.

*

"YOU HAVE A visitor," Trixie announced, standing in Nan's office doorway first thing the following morning.

Nan pointed to the phone she was holding up to her ear, indicating that she was in the middle of a call.

"No, you don't have to call anybody. You have an actual visitor here now. To see you," Trixie repeated.

Nan sighed, asked her caller if she could call back later, and acquiesced. Trixie was not going to let up until that visitor was admitted that very second; she could tell. What a one-track mind.

Sophia Sardone walked in, bringing with her a faint scent of lemons and flowers. Wow, she smelled good. Wow, she looked good. Nan had often thought about her since meeting her at Joe's funeral. But she could never figure out how to bump into a funeral home director casually. Go browse her casket selection? Go to random funerals just to catch a glimpse of her?

She looked a little nervous. Nan wondered why.

"I wanted to thank you, to tell you that you changed my daughter's life," Sophia began, leaning in.

Oh. She has a daughter. Probably married. To a man.

"She went to your glassblowing program. They picked her to blow a glass ornament in front of the crowd. She came home a completely different person. Now she wants to be an artist. She's determined to be one, in fact. I've never seen her passionate about anything like this. She's studying art books; she's been back to the glass museum five times so far; she found an art class; and most of all, she is deliriously happy. She had been terribly sad about my divorce."

Divorce. Ding, ding, ding.

When the moment expanded to Sophia's bashful confession that she'd been angling to meet Nan, hoping not only to thank her but also to ask her out on an honest-to-god date, Nan felt herself jump off the ground for an instant, levitated by joy.

She had the crazy notion Joe had sent Sophia here and pictured Joe grinning at her, giving her his thumbs-up, go-ahead signal. That man knew what it was to enjoy a moment fully. That man knew what it was to find love.

*

FOR THEIR FIRST date, they went out to dinner at a Japanese restaurant a few towns away that Sophia suggested. Nan's avocado sushi fell apart as usual, her ineptitude with chopsticks the same as always. Why did she even try to use them? How in the world did Sophia pull that off, the elegant swooping in and capturing those tiny little strands of rice? It must be that her beautiful long fingers worked better for chopsticks than Nan's stubby little ones. Sophia saw her difficulties and without remarking on it or slowing down the flow of words between them, gestured to the server for a fork.

They talked about the library; for Nan, it was rare that people talked to a librarian without feeling they had to boast how long it had been since they'd been in a library or apologize for their reading tastes. Did people feel compelled to confess to hair stylists at a party how long it had been since their last haircut or dye job? She didn't think so.

So why did people feel the need to immediately

announce their reading proclivities to librarians (who hadn't asked)? She had heard it all: I don't read. I only read fantasy. I never read novels. I only read military history. I only read magazines. I haven't read a book since high school.

It was genuinely funny to Nan. She never had any kind of response to make. Should she absolve them when they confessed, as if she were a priest? Assign them to read outside their chosen categories and limits? Go forth and sin no more. For your penance, read the top ten Booker Prize nominees in literary fiction. For your penance, read a poem a night for an entire year.

Sophia read in bed every night (Nan shivered at the image). "Whatever catches my eye, I'm eclectic that way," she said. "I browse in bookstores in Philly and New York or wherever I'm traveling, always have a stack waiting, but I don't rush through books. I take my time."

Nan didn't share the bookstore offer with her. That felt like too much, too soon. She wanted to ease into this as if she were sliding into a warm bath. She wanted to get to know Sophia little by little, to prolong the pleasure. She wanted Sophia to know her deeply, and that took time.

Everything Sophia said landed in Nan with a warm bump. Not a fireworks explosion, but a lovely simmer. Sophia was a steady flashing green light of a woman. It was so basic; Nan had learned in kindergarten that green meant go, red meant stop. But her whole life until now, she had ignored the red lights of the women in her past, hoping they would magically turn green. Even at fifty years old, when T came along flashing FUN but with huge red lights surrounding it, Nan had blithely followed the fun and ignored the inevitable disappointment ahead.

When someone shows you who they are, believe them the first time, Maya Angelou said, that most wise and wondrous writer. Nan was embarrassed at how long it had taken her to get it, when all she had to do was search out the green lights and go, go, go.

They talked about the rivalry, dating back decades, between Sophia's funeral home and Bongiovani's. "The truth is, there's plenty of business to go around." She laughed. "We're good friends; we help each other out. But people enjoy a good drama, a story of who undercut who, who beat out the other."

The dinner lasted a long time. When Nan kissed her goodnight and went home, all she could think about was kissing her again and again for a very long time. Soon, she hoped.

CHAPTER THIRTY-NINE

"IN MY LINE of work, I see a lot of interrupted lives," Sophia said.

They had been talking about how life threw curveballs, how people made plans and then had to duck and switch directions, how fast it could all happen. It was their second date; they were on a moonlight walk through the woods. Sophia knew a section where the owls hung out. If you were lucky, she said, you could hear a screech owl singing.

"Not hooting?"

"They sing too, in this funny way, like a horse whinny. And they make clacking and hissing sounds. It's wild."

Nan thought about Joe's interrupted life, how he went for a walk in the moonlight and never came home again. Or was it interrupted? For a man terrified of hospitals, maybe dying instantly at the foot of a tree was the best possible death at the end of a long life.

"So I try not to think too far ahead." Sophia stopped and put her finger to her lips. The owls were nearby.

What a perfect thing to say. Sophia didn't even know about the bookstore, and she still managed to say the exact thing Nan needed to hear.

All Nan had to do was focus on her next step.

*

IT WAS DUSK when Nan opened the door to the apartment above the shoe repair shop for the first time.

The apartment was completely empty. She moved around in it and stood still in each room, turning on all the lights as she went. There was a slight motion in the air as if the rooms responded to her presence there. She loved the feeling of being perched over Main Street.

The wood floors were shiny and gorgeous in their imperfection. She noticed traces of the people who had lived there—dark circles where someone had dropped a lit cigarette or from a wood ember from the fireplace, scratches of a heavy old armoire being moved, a hollow spot (a tiny secret hiding place?) where she felt her foot sink down.

The doors were framed by beautifully carved wood, reminding Nan of a museum made from an old house, the kind where you spend as much time looking at the building as you do the contents. She ran her finger along the grooves for the pleasure of it. She hadn't expected such beauty and grace above a worn old shop, but here it was.

She guessed the kitchen was straight out of the 1940s, with its painted yellow cabinets with red knobs and handles. She loved it exactly as it was. What did she care about the latest and greatest kitchen stuff, she who never cooked? All she would use in here was the refrigerator.

The windows were amazingly long and wide, taking up half the front wall. On the opposite corner—Main Street and First Avenue—was the showpiece building of the town. Painted in flashy gold accents, it resembled a plump society lady with a lot of jewelry on her bosom.

Nan had been walking by it for months, but from the street level, she'd never appreciated the elaborate pressed metal decorations in seashells and floral designs or the triangle cornice on the roof as ornate as a tiara. Now that she was on the same level, she was wowed by all the special touches.

Chuck had told her that, over the decades, the building had, in turn, housed a dry goods store, an ice cream parlor, and even an automobile showroom back when cars were new-fangled inventions. Now, it was a massive antique and secondhand furniture store that people came from all over to visit.

If I live here, I will furnish this apartment from that store. I won't rush, either. Each piece will be exactly right, even if it takes a long time to find it.

At fifty years old, she had never lived in a place that was wholly her own. She'd gone from her family home to college, then to a long series of rented and shared apartments. She had never owned a place of her own, never even thought it was possible.

This place could be my home.

Just then, she saw a woman in the apartment above the furniture store moving from room to room, turning on lights and closing her drapes to the night. The woman saw Nan and raised her hand in greeting, the surprise giving Nan a little warm jolt. She was holding something with one arm. Was that a baby? A doll? No, it was a hefty white-bellied cat. The woman raised the cat's arm and made it wave at Nan too.

Oh, a cat. A longing to hold one barreled over Nan. She had loved cats ever since childhood; they'd always had one in their home. After her mom died, their last cat, Lydia, would sit on Nan's lap and pat her with one paw when Nan cried. She'd never told anyone about that, thinking it sounded unbelievable that a cat could know the pain of a human and try to comfort with touch. It was true though. She could still remember how amazing the communication had felt flowing between them, with no words.

After she left home, Nan's lifetime of renting and moving so often made it too hard for her to have a cat. And it was expensive to feed cats, take them to the vet, and buy litter. She could hardly keep herself; a cat was a luxury she couldn't afford.

But if she owned this whole building, if this apartment were all hers, she could have a cat. Her favorite bookstores always had a cat perched on shelves or jumping down to surprise people browsing. Come to think of it, even her favorite hair salon had a cat that coolly eyed customers in the mirror during haircuts and, if you were lucky, would leap into your lap with a purr.

A cat of her own. A bookstore cat who came upstairs after work with her every day. The thought thrilled her. All she had to do was say yes to make it all happen.

Cat Lady was the ultimate cliché and frequent put-down directed toward older women, she acknowledged.

Guess what, world. I. JUST. DON'T. CARE.

I. WANT. CAT.

She'd rushed into things her whole life though. She was determined to give this time enough to be sure. Chuck would have to wait.

*

HOLDING HANDS WITH Sophia. The warm current pulsing between them. The pleasure of swinging along together around the farmers' market. All decisions on hold. Nan couldn't think about anything but this woman. Being with Sophia had the effect of pushing everything right out of Nan's head. This was what it meant to stay right in the present moment. Because when the present moment was humming with joy running around in her body, where else would her mind go? Nowhere. She was staying with this fantastic feeling. She was plugged in.

"Hey, book woman." T stood in front of them, grinning.

Two of my favorite words. Book. Woman. That's my whole life, captured in those words.

Nan kind of loved T's new nickname for her. She was relieved to find that she felt no residual lust; she had avoided T for months, just in case. After all, the body wanted what the body wanted. Plenty of book plots and real-life stories attested to that.

"Do you know Sophia?" Nan asked.

"Everyone knows Sophia," T said, punching Sophia lightly in the shoulder.

Oh no, was there a history there? Nan shot a look at Sophia, who seemed to read her mind. She rolled her eyes at Nan.

I'll take that as a no.

Sophia hated to talk about the past. It was one of the things Nan loved best about her. All she had said about her marriage was that she'd "fallen pregnant" while in college, jokily using the British term. It *was* funny, as if a baby was a random occurrence that had just landed on her, unbidden. Nan didn't know if she was Sophia's first female lover or her fiftieth, and that was absolutely fine with her.

In huge contrast, Nan remembered many awful first dates in her past, where the woman would immediately launch into a litany of her exes and why they broke up. When one date started imitating her ex's predilection for babytalk in bed

(EWWWW), Nan had excused herself, pretending to go to the bathroom, and exited the restaurant altogether. There had been no point in going on from there.

Later, when Sophia was off talking to a friend, T ran back up to Nan to whisper, "Hey, you owe me. You were wound up tight when you got to town. I loosened you up for her."

So crude. So true.

Nan didn't want to admit that out loud. She didn't like the picture of herself it unspooled in her mind: T as a cowpoke who had lassoed her to the ground and tamed her for other riders.

*

WHAT WERE THOSE ghastly, unnerving sounds? Wildebeests mating. Monster truck rally. Howling banshees. Wolverines in heat. Big rigs racing. Trapped demons. Cyclones in an elevator. Death match of bulls. Wall-shaking giants' brawl.

Sophia snores. My gorgeous, sexy woman snores.

It was 3:00 a.m. Nan raised herself on her elbow to look. Was it really true those sounds were coming out of that beautiful face?

She had to get out of this room immediately. There must be a couch she could crash on for a few hours and stop the throbbing in her ears. Then she could creep back into bed with Sophia as if she'd never left. She grabbed her backpack, tiptoed to the hall, and closed the bedroom door behind her.

Please let Sophia's daughter still be out for the evening. Please don't let her see me standing here naked in the hallway, fishing out a T-shirt and underpants.

It was her first time in Sophia's rambling old house, so she didn't even remember where the living room was exactly. Thankfully, she didn't live above the funeral home itself or Nan would have nowhere to go to get away from the sounds, except to the dearly departed. Sophia's cousin Sal lived above the funeral home as second-in-command of the family business.

All she wanted was a couch to collapse on so she could summon up all the wonderful memories of this first night together and shove the racket out of her brain. She found one and curled up under a warm throw. Her body felt quite wonderful. If only her ears would stop throbbing.

Just as her eyes finally closed, she heard the front door open across the hallway. When a whoosh of fresh air hit her face, she cracked open her eyes to see Rae, Sophia's daughter, standing over her with a big toothy grin on her face.

The first time they met, Nan could not believe how little

resemblance there was between mother and daughter. While Sophia moved with grace and calmness streaming out of her, Rae was a spinning top of wild energy and frenetic motion. Sophia's face had the classic features of a 1940s movie star. Rae's face was round as an acorn; she was a little nuthead with bright eyes.

The noise from above was far away but still audible. Rae covered her ears and fake-screamed. "The beast comes in the night to chase the magic sleep away. That's how I think of her snoring—the beast is back."

"Is it always this way?" Nan was afraid to hear the answer.

For the love of all that is holy, tell me this is a rare occurrence.

"Oh, yeah." Rae grinned. "Can I tell you how incredibly happy I am to be leaving for college? If my roommate plays loud music all night, I won't even care. If she has dramatic fights with her boyfriend or girlfriend at 3:00 a.m., I will roll right over. If a dance party erupts at midnight on the floor above mine, it won't faze me a bit. Nothing could top this, am I right?"

"There's no remedy? No fix?"

"She's tried them all. Nothing works. Her nose is decorative only, a totally nonfunctional feature. I'm surprised she didn't warn you. But she forgets. She honestly has no idea how bad it is for the rest of us."

Rae opened a drawer and pulled out a pair of noise-cancelling earphones for Nan. "Because I like you, because I love my unbearable racket of a mother, I bequeath these to you with my very best wishes. I'll be waving goodnight to you both soon, from my quiet college dorm far, far away."

All these surprises in life kept barreling at Nan, bundled together. The thrill of discovering Sophia's body tied up with the cacophony that was the price of actually sleeping with her. The humiliation of the Provincetown failure followed by the exhilaration of a job proposition she'd never envisioned.

This town seemed to bring newness her way constantly. She had read about geographic locations that served as a life nexus, connecting past and present, spirit and body. But they were always glamorous, exotic places like Sedona, a vortex for higher powers and ecstatic experiences. Where you could sit on a hill at dawn and connect to the universe in a rainbow haze. Where you could find peace and balance. Where healing from pain and losses flowed through you and transformed your life.

Vortexes were never set in places like New Jersey, which mean-spirited jesters called the Armpit of America. But why not? This vortex seemed to be whirling around Nan for a rea-son.

CHAPTER FORTY

"ARE YOU A ninny?" Immaculata pulled a blackened pepper from the gas flame and put it into a brown paper bag with the others to soften.

"Not that I know of." Nan handed her the cutting board full of the raw red peppers she had been halving. Her mind was preoccupied; had she cut the peppers the wrong way, causing Immaculata's ire?

"A man gives you a building, you take it."

Nan dropped her knife on the floor. "Who told you that?"

Immaculata pursed her lips, shrugged. "I hear things. A

man hands over a business to you, you take it. A place to live, no rent, all yours. Snap it up."

Nan picked up the knife and put it in the sink. She wasn't going to stand there and take this.

"Don't be stupid. That's all I'm saying." Immaculata ripped the burnt skin off the pepper and dropped the warm pepper into a bowl with garlic and olive oil.

"It's absolutely none of your business." Nan turned to leave.

"What's wrong with you? Is your head up your ass or what?" Immaculata picked up a roll and threw it at Nan.

Nan screamed at the surprise of it. "You crazy old broad." She grabbed the bag of rolls and aimed them one by one at Immaculata's head. Immaculata ducked and thwacked the rolls back at Nan with the cutting board.

When they stopped laughing and sat down to face each other across the table, momentarily exhausted, Nan said, "I don't need you to tell me what to do. I know exactly what to do."

She surprised herself with that, but it was very clear. She could feel the pulsing inner guidance directing her. Unmistakable.

*

NAN ORDERED A Virgin Mary at the diner, batting away the memory of the giant Mary statue rolling down Main Street. This was just a lovely mocktail, seasoned tomato juice with no vodka but with extra olives and celery, exactly what she needed. If there was ever a day to keep her wits about her, this was that day.

Her brain was as lit up as a pinball machine, her thoughts racing around like those little balls; when they landed in the right spot, she felt her eye sockets light up and her eyeballs roll around just like a real pinball goddess.

She and Chuck faced each other across their favorite highway diner booth. He felt so familiar to her, the brother she didn't have in real life. As if they had spent many meals together in previous lifetimes.

A baby in the next booth popped up suddenly and shrieked at them, clearly thrilled by his newfound ability to pull himself up to standing. His laugh was so mirthful and irresistible that soon the whole corner of the diner was laughing with him. Chuck played peekaboo to egg him on.

Then that silly, dear man jumped out of his seat and knelt right on the floor, blocking the aisle, with both hands crossed over his heart. The servers froze. The other diners stopped talking. The cashier craned her head to see them more clearly, waving people away who were waiting to pay. It was clear to Nan they thought this was a marriage proposal. She laughed out loud at how far off base they all were.

The crowd looked at her and then at Chuck, heads swiveling as they held their collective breath, waiting. Nan had never before considered how extremely embarrassing it would feel to be in the actual position of being proposed to publicly.

"Will you do it, Nan? Will you open a bookstore with me?" Chuck pleaded.

Their server, two plates lined up on her arm, burst out of the kitchen and headed for them. When she saw Chuck on his knees, she stopped so fast her shoes screeched like an old car when the brakes were slammed on.

Nan shook her head emphatically NO, and the whole diner said *Ohhhh* in sad unison and picked up their forks. Chuck got up from his knees, rubbing them, and slumped back in his seat. The server laid their plates down hard, glaring at Nan.

"It's not me," Nan said. "I'm not the one."

He simply listened. He had a wife and daughter; he knew

better than to try to argue her out of it. That was obvious.

"Your offer is so generous, Chuck. Your vision is so clear. But my heart isn't in it. Because I am suddenly possessed with my own vision and a counterproposal for you."

He nodded, waiting.

First things first. "I love the apartment so much. I want to rent it, make it my home," she said. "I do NOT want to own the building. It's too much. It makes me cringe thinking of it."

"Yes. The apartment is all yours. I would love for you to live there," Chuck said instantly.

The joy of that. The absolute rightness of it too. This was the first time in her life she had fallen in love with a place, walked into a space that put its arms around her and plainly said *You're home.*

Now for the rest of it. Nervous excitement mounted, a bubbly combination that made her feel as high as champagne.

"Chuck, what this town desperately needs is a new library building. You know all the reasons, I'm sure. For one, it's a former jail and still looks like one. Sends the wrong message. A library is the heart and soul of a town; it deserves the very best."

She went on to describe her vision of Brand New! Glass front! One story! Welcoming! Fully accessible! Zippy front door that whooshed open automatically, signaling *Hello You, Come Right In*! Gorgeous, light filled, art filled! Where community groups would flock to meet. Where every reader had a seat. Where fantastic programs would be held. Where books could twirl around and strut their beautiful selves on ample shelves. A computer lab! Information literacy and English as a Second Language classroom! A Children's Room with no bars on the windows! An outside reading room in a sculpture garden! She caught her breath finally and stopped.

"But what does this have to do with my storefront?" Chuck looked bewildered.

Nan laughed. She had been getting ahead of herself in her excitement. "I propose that it become a non-profit fundraising arm for the new library. The Friends of the Library can run a giant used bookstore there and donate all the book proceeds to the building campaign. I know the perfect person to run it—Lolly. She needs a job, and you need a manager. She can organize volunteers to keep it open seven days a week, just like a real bookstore. It's largely symbolic, of course. There's no way a bunch of used books can bring in enough money for a new building. But it would make everyone aware of the building campaign and get people involved in a tangible way. In the meantime, I'll be writing grant proposals for federal and state construction funds for ten years or so and begging the town council to get on board and all that jazz."

Chuck's eyes bulged; he took a big gulp of air and choked out, "I have the land."

What was he talking about?

"I have the perfect lot for a new library. Right in town. An abandoned factory burned down there years ago, leaving an empty lot a whole block long just sitting there. I've been holding on to it for years because I knew it was destined for something really important. I just didn't know what. This is it. I will donate the land."

And just like that, years were knocked off the timeline. Land was so expensive and rare around here, in a town that had been built up since the 1800s.

"I was going to sink a lot of money into my bookstore idea," Chuck continued. "So instead, I'll get the accountant to funnel it to the new library fund. It will be a good chunk of what we need to get us started anyway. I have buddies who will contribute too. They always need tax deductions."

Nan had always thought that jaws didn't really drop open—what a stupid expression—but her jaw had dropped open as if it was hinged. She forced her mouth back together before she asked, "You have secret millionaire buddies?"

"I can neither confirm nor deny that." He grinned.

A wild elation began to build in her body, rising up from the core of her. "But what about your bookstore dream?"

"Dreams are not all meant to come true, I guess." He sighed. "I'm an addict, so it's probably for the best anyway. Libraries I can handle. But if I had a whole store full of fresh new books, I'd never go home. I'd be one of those bookstore guys who lives there, wearing out the best chair in the place, high from new book fumes."

"This won't be easy," Nan warned. "We have years of work ahead of us to pull this off. Are you in?"

"Oh, I'm all the way in," he said.

"One more thing."

He leaned forward, took a sip of coffee.

"Can I have a cat in my new apartment? I need cat. I want cat. I must have cat," she said.

He spit out his coffee, laughing, and nodded. Just then, Sophia walked in; how unplanned and absolutely perfect. As Nan waved her over, the baby in the next booth shrieked with glee and hurled a syrup-sticky coin that landed smack in the middle of Nan's forehead and magically stayed there. Chuck pointed to it, named her Nickel Nan.

In the future, he would shorten her nickname to Nickel and claim that when he saw money fly across the room and stick to her, he knew the library building project was a winner, and that was when he donated the land. It all happened but not in that order and not for that reason, but such was the nature of all good stories, which morphed with each retelling and got better as they grew.

As for the coin on her forehead, well, Nan *had* begged the universe for change. She just had no idea the vast intelligence that runs the world was quite so literal. Amazing.

Acknowledgements

I am very grateful to my expert editor, Elizabetta McKay, for her sharp insights, excellent skills, and wise guidance, and to Raevyn and the whole team at NineStar Press for championing LGBTQA voices and stories.

It is an incredible gift in my life to have Sara Pritchard as an early reader of my writing for so many years; her friendship is an even greater gift.

For a writer, the world of the public library is a playground of wonderfulness, and I am thankful to have spent many years working in them and meeting all kinds of readers. I salute my former library colleagues and appreciate our time together.

I am inspired by British novelist Barbara Pym's books full of sly humor and small triumphs in life.

Most of all, I am grateful for my life with Jackie Warren, my wife and my everything.

ABOUT KATHY ANDERSON

Kathy Anderson is the author of the short story collection, *Bull and Other Stories* (Autumn House Press), which was a finalist for the Lambda Literary Awards for Lesbian Fiction, Publishing Triangle's Edmund White Award for Debut Fiction, and Foreword INDIES Book of the Year in Short Stories. *The New Town Librarian* is her first novel. Kathy holds a Master of Library Science degree and worked as a librarian for over twenty-five years in small-town public libraries in southern New Jersey. Her home is in Philadelphia, Pennsylvania, where she lives with her wife, who is her exact opposite in every way and therefore her perfect match.

Email
kathyandersonwriter@yahoo.com

Facebook
www.facebook.com/kathyandersonwriter1

Twitter
@anderson_kathy

Website
www.Kathyandersonwriter.com

Instagram
www.instagram.com/anderson_kathy_writer

Linktree
www.linktr.ee/kathyandersonwriter

CONNECT WITH NINESTAR PRESS

WWW.NINESTARPRESS.COM

WWW.FACEBOOK.COM/NINESTARPRESS

WWW.FACEBOOK.COM/GROUPS/NINESTARNICHE

WWW.TWITTER.COM/NINESTARPRESS

WWW.INSTAGRAM.COM/NINESTARPRESS

CPSIA information can be obtained
at www.ICGtesting.com
Printed in the USA
LVHW021542270423
745406LV00006B/106

9 781648 906084